W9-CPF-628

# The Girl from Atlantis

# The Girl from Atlantis

By Richard Schenkman

Illustrated by Humberto Braga

GMI Books
Los Angeles, California

Text copyright © 2009 by Richard Schenkman
Illustrations copyright © 2009 by Humberto Braga

Second Printing 2012

An edition of 300 numbered, slipcased copies has also been published, signed by the author and illustrator.

Schenkman, Richard
The Girl From Atlantis / Richard Schenkman ;
illustrated by Humberto Braga. – 1st ed.

Summary: Athena Crowley is an 11-year-old girl who lives at the Atlantis Resort in the Bahamas, where her father discovered the mythical Lost City for which it is named. Her life changes when an old turtle starts talking to her, and Athena realizes she can communicate with sea creatures. Determined to understand her roots, Athena takes a risky journey to the undersea kingdom of Atlantica, where mer-people rule, humans are slaves, and dangerous and thrilling surprises await her.

ISBN: 978-0-9841809-0-5   (hardcover)
         978-0-9841809-1-2   (limited edition)

Library of Congress Control Number:  2009907931

Printed in China

This book was typeset in Times New Roman.
The illustrations were done in Graphite and Digital.

www.thegirlfromatlantis.com

*Atlantis…*
*According to legend, it was an island city*
*created and ruled by*
*the Greek god Poseidon, and named for*
*his first-born son, Atlas.*
*Some believe it to have been the most advanced*
*culture of ancient times, destroyed by angry gods*
*when the people became corrupt.*
*Some even believe the greatest achievements of*
*ancient man – aqueducts, pyramids, democracy –*
*all came from Atlantis and spread to Europe and*
*Asia in the decades before the city was destroyed.*

For Tiger

# Chapter 1

Athena Crowley was only two years old the first time she should have drowned.

She was on a little sailboat with her mother and father when she tumbled right over the side. She slipped into the water with barely a splash and sank like a stone.

And yet she did not die.

Even at two, Athena was already a strong swimmer. She had first learned to swim at only six months, long before she could walk. She would crawl along the side of a pool and drop her body into the water, to the great amusement of her parents and the consternation of the hotel's guests.

"The baby!" someone would cry out, quickly rising from their chaise lounge to rescue her, but she would already be giggling and paddling along the surface of the water towards her father's welcoming arms.

The person would settle back into their chair, shaking their head disapprovingly at the way an irresponsible young father could let his toddler frighten strangers so, even while being impressed with the child's abilities all the same.

Consequently, Athena refused to wear a life jacket, even out on the ocean, and her parents, confident in her aquatic skills, gave up trying to force one upon her.

# Chapter 2

The day of the accident was such a warm, beautiful, sunny day there hadn't been much of a discussion about piling into the small family sailboat and heading out into the surf. It was something they did several times a week – whenever they could, really, and especially on days like this.

In the moments before it happened, Athena's father, Robert, was securing the rigging, having just come about. Her mother, Irina, was up in the bow, eyes closed, enjoying the sensation of warm sun and sea spray on her face. Something told Irina to check on her daughter, so she opened her eyes and turned to see Athena sitting on her little seat, watching Robert work. Irina smiled, closed her eyes again and turned her face once more into the breeze. There was a good, strong wind and the boat was slicing quickly through the water.

Something caught Athena's attention out of the corner of her eye. Something big, and silvery. She thought, *What was that?* She turned herself around, not quite kneeling on the bench, and peered into the water rushing by. *Maybe it's a mermaid!*

Like many people who live by the ocean, Athena had an abiding interest in mermaids. She'd grown up hearing stories of mermaids and mermen, of mythical sea creatures of every size and stripe.

Athena and her parents lived in the Bahamas, a nation of some 800 islands in the blue Caribbean Sea. Her home was on Paradise Island, a long, narrow strip of sand and palm trees which sits alongside the much larger island of New Providence, where the capital city of Nassau is located.

Nearly all the grownups on Paradise Island worked at the Atlantis, a giant resort hotel which occupied most of the island. Robert Crowley was a marine archeologist who worked there since before the place was even built. Indeed, he was the person who had discovered traces of the original, mythical, "lost city" of Atlantis for which the hotel was named. Robert was fiercely intelligent; you could tell from one look into his flashing hazel eyes. His long nose had a bump or two from youthful misadventures, but he was still a handsome man.

Robert had been on the island a few years when he met Irina, a local woman from a fishing village. She was kind and beautiful, with brown skin and shiny black hair. He always said that she had a smile to light up a room and the next room over as well. He fell in love with her at first sight, and married her as soon as he could. And less than two years after their wedding, Athena was born. That was nearly three years ago.

Athena looked a lot like her mother, except that her long wavy hair was brown, with golden tips courtesy of the sun. People always told her she had Robert's chin, but she wasn't sure how that could be. "Then what's at the bottom of his face?" she would ask.

Robert and Irina named their daughter after a goddess…

According to ancient legend, the original Athena defeated Poseidon in a contest to determine which one of them would become the patron god of a Grecian city. The challenge was to present the citizens with the gift they liked the most. Poseidon thought he had the game won when he caused a spring to flow forth from the ground. But the water was salty, and nobody liked drinking it. Athena gave them an olive tree, which produced a very useful and delicious food.

Needless to say, Athena won the contest and the city of Athens was named after her. Having lost, Poseidon grew angry and threw a fit, causing a giant flood. He went back down to his watery kingdom where he stayed until years later, when he founded the legendary island city of Atlantis.

Living at the Atlantis resort, Athena was surrounded by sea life and by rare artifacts from ancient civilizations… and living by the ocean, there was always the chance that a mermaid would appear. Athena's father would patiently remind her that mermaids weren't real, but her mother would wink and point out that you never knew what was real and what wasn't. "After all," she said, "wasn't the Lost City of Atlantis just a myth until your father discovered it?"

# Chapter 3

Athena stared into the water intently, hoping the fish – or mermaid – would swim by again. Looking into the clear blue, she saw tiny flicks of silver and yellow. It was a school of baby jacks. Peering deeper, she could discern the outline of a large coral formation. And then… *there it was again!*

It was big, whatever it was, and fast, swimming rapidly alongside the boat about ten feet below the surface. It kept perfect pace with the small craft. Athena's heart was racing, too. She'd give anything to meet a mermaid.

Athena leaned over the side, stretching out a hand. Normally she was too small to reach the water this way, but the boat was listing due to the strong wind. Just as her fingertips touched the surface, the creature came closer. *If that's a fish*, she thought, *it's a big one. So maybe it really is a --*

She was about to turn and ask her dad to take a look at the creature when the boat hit a bump – an errant wave is all it was – and over she went. Just like that. She was so startled, she didn't even have time to be scared.

Robert Crowley was nearly knocked over by the bump. "Whoa," he smiled. "Is everybody okay?"
He looked around and didn't see his daughter.
"Athena?"

Irina heard the panic in his voice and opened her eyes, instantly scanning in every direction.

Robert sharply turned the boat into the wind, stopping it dead in its tracks. He listened carefully, but heard only the wind and waves. He shouted, "Athena!" No answer.

He leapt across the boat to where she had been sitting, and stared back toward the direction from which they'd come. Were those bubbles breaking the surface?

He grabbed the rudder and steered the boat back against the wind, willing the craft toward the spot where he'd seen bubbles. He turned it sharply once again, quickly dropped the sail, grabbed his face mask, and threw himself into the water. He tried to not panic, to stay calm and in control of himself, but his heart was pounding.

Meanwhile Irina grabbed a rope and tied off the main sail, and then worked on setting the anchor.

Robert held his breath and looked around desperately for any sign of his daughter. He knew he had only a few precious seconds before she'd run out of air, lose consciousness, and drown.

Luckily it was a sunny day, and the water was only about thirty feet deep. Robert could therefore see everything in the area quite clearly. But he couldn't see Athena. He jetted back toward the surface.

"See anything?" he called out to Irina.
She shook her head, and shouted, "I'll check out the other side!" Irina stood up on the starboard railing and dove into the water.

Robert took another deep breath and surface-dove as far down as he could. Perhaps Athena was caught on a coral…

Robert sensed a flash behind him, just at the edge of his periphery. He spun to find a huge, shimmering barracuda, its razor-sharp teeth practically glowing in the sunlight. The fish was at least four feet long – bigger than Athena! He knew in his head that the animal posed no immediate danger to him or his family, but it was terrifying nevertheless.

It was just hovering there, staring at him, its round silver eye unblinking.

As Robert watched the barracuda a moment longer, he saw two air bubbles rise up just past its head. He instinctively looked down – and there was Athena! Her eyes were closed, and she appeared to be resting peacefully on a small reef. A tiny bubble of air emerged from her nose.

He raced toward her and in a moment held her in his arms. He swam to the surface and had her inside the boat in seconds.

He pulled off his face mask and listened; it didn't sound like she was breathing.
"Athena," he said, quietly but firmly. "Athena!" he repeated, a bit louder. He snapped his fingers, tapped her cheek, but she did not respond.

Robert laid her carefully on the floor of the boat, and tilted her head back. He checked her mouth – there were no obstructions. Trembling, but staying as calm as he could, he closed her nostrils with the thumb and index finger of his left hand, and opened her mouth with his right. He put his mouth over hers, and breathed into her lungs.

Her little chest rose and fell, but she did not respond. He did it again, but still, she did not start breathing.

Robert placed his hands firmly on her chest and pressed sharply down and up.
"One – two, one – two, one – two – "

By this time Irina had surfaced again. She called out, "Robert!"
"I have her!" He continued the chest compressions.
"How is she?"
"I'm doing CPR."

Irina climbed back into the boat as Robert did more compressions. He whispered desperately into Athena's ear, "Please wake up, darling. Please, Athena." Once more he closed her nose and breathed into her mouth –

With a sputtering cough, Athena awoke. Her lungs had been full of water and it all came out now, through her mouth and nose. She sat up quickly, blinking hard, and looking around.

"Daddy! Where... what happened?"
"You fell into the water, darling. You nearly drowned. This is why I'm always telling you to wear a life – "
"Did you see the fish, daddy? The big silver one?"
Robert was surprised by the question. "I... yes, I did. There was a large barracuda."
"He was really nice, wasn't he?"
"I – I wouldn't know."
"He told me not to be scared. He said he wouldn't hurt me. And I wasn't scared! I wasn't scared at all."

Robert looked intently at his daughter. She'd clearly had some kind of hallucination as she was drowning. Maybe it was the oxygen deprivation that caused her to imagine the fish talking to her. He looked up at Irina, who was standing by the gunwale. She smiled at him and shrugged:

"She says a barracuda told her not to be afraid?"

Robert nodded.

"Well, he'd know, wouldn't he?"

Robert laughed, but overcome with relief and emotion, he found he was crying instead. He hugged Athena tight. "I'm just so glad you're safe. I don't know what I would have done if something had -- " He broke off, unable to speak.

# Chapter 4

Over the next few months, Irina kept an especially close eye on Athena, as though she might vanish any minute. She seemed to believe that her daughter's survival had been some kind of mistake an unknown authority would soon correct, arriving to take the girl away in a flash.

But no one came, and life went on as before.

Robert continued diving with his crew, finding new artifacts from ancient Atlantis, restoring them, cataloguing them, and putting them on display. He met with experts from around the world, learned men and women who wanted to solve the age old mysteries as much as he did. With their help, he even began to translate the hieroglyphs carved into many of the pieces, rediscovering the long-dead language of the Atlanteans.

Athena enjoyed life at the resort, sliding down slides, joining poolside games, learning about the creatures of the sea. Her favorite ride was The Serpent: you climbed all the way to the top of the Mayan Temple and clambered into a giant inner tube. Next, a rush of water pushed you down a pitch-dark, twisty-turny tunnel where you never knew what was coming next. Finally, you splashed into the daylight surrounded by man-eating sharks!

Really, you were safely inside a clear plastic tunnel, but as you floated towards the small lagoon at the end of the ride, you were surrounded by more than dozen huge gray reef sharks.

Even though Athena had been down the slide countless times, she still giggled and squealed with delight the same way all the visitors did. She loved the speed, the exciting mix of darkness and light, and of course, sharks.

Irina tried to get Athena to talk about her experience under water the day of the accident. She wanted to learn more about Athena's odd feeling that a fish had spoken to her. But Athena's memory of the details quickly faded, brushed away by the shock of it all and a raft of new adventures. So Irina did her best to put it behind her, too, and mostly succeeded.

On the day of Athena's third birthday, Robert skipped work and the family went out for a big breakfast. Athena had waffles with berries and the biggest pile of whipped cream anyone had ever seen. She had a chocolate brownie, too. It was all very decadent... that's what the waitress called it, anyway.

Smiling broadly, her little face covered with foamy cream, Athena said, "This is the best birthday ever. Thank you so much!"

Robert leaned back in his chair. "We have presents for you too, you know."
"Really?"
"Sure. Mine first?"

Athena nodded her head up and down, thrilled, as Robert presented a wrapped parcel about the size of a cigar box.

Athena tore the wrapping paper to scraps, revealing an old book. She held it up, staring at the cover. She couldn't read the title, but knew it started with a "T".

On the cover there was a large color painting of a one-legged sailor with a young boy on the deck of an old-fashioned ship.

"T…r…" she said.

"Treasure Island, honey," Robert interrupted. "It's one of the greatest books ever written. My grandpa gave it to my dad when he was a kid, my dad gave it to me, and now it's your turn. It's got pirates, treasure, rum, swordfights… everything!"
"You'll read it to me?"
"Starting tonight, angel."

Athena jumped up from her seat and ran around to kiss her dad. She loved it when he read stories to her.

Irina presented a small gift box. "It's your first piece of jewelry. There'll be more later on, I'm sure."

Athena opened the box carefully. It was lined with black satin, and sitting in the center was a small silver heart on a chain. Athena's eyes went wide. "It's beautiful!"
"Open it up."
"What do you mean?"

Irina gently took the locket and popped it open with her fingernail. There were two tiny photographs inside; on the left, Athena as a little baby, and on the right, a picture of Irina Robert had snapped just a few weeks before.

Athena placed her hand on her mother's and very dramatically said, "I love it. I'll never take it off."
Irina laughed and said, "Well, maybe in the bath. And certainly when you're going down those slides!"

# Chapter 5

They would spend the rest of the day – where else? – out on the little sailboat. It was a glorious day; perfect sailing weather. They would swim, and Robert even had a mind to do a little fishing. If they were really lucky, he'd snag their dinner while relaxing on the boat.

There was a good breeze and so they sailed quickly out from the small pier into the open water. Athena was always happy to get away from the noisy jet skis and the scary parasailers. She and her parents were happy to see the visitors enjoying themselves, but they preferred the peace and isolation out at sea.

As the wind died, the boat slowed and stopped. Robert said, "What do you think? Good a place as any?"
Irina licked her finger and stuck it up into the air. "Unless we start paddling, we're not going anywhere else any time soon," she laughed.

Robert crossed the boat to join Athena, who was sitting back in the stern. "Whaddya say, kid, help me get the rod ready?"
Athena nodded. Irina was up in the bow of the boat. She slipped off her shoes, and started securing the mainsail.

Suddenly, the sky turned from blue to black in an in instant, and a terrible storm appeared from nowhere. Robert huddled tightly with Athena, thinking it was impossible how quickly the weather had changed.

The waves abruptly swelled five, six feet high and water splashed over the sides of the boat. Irina tried to join her husband and daughter, crossing hand-over-hand along the gunwale, but the wind and blinding rain pinned her down.

Now the boom broke free and swung wildly from side to side. A huge gust of wind nearly blew the boat over, forcing the boom to spin around a full 360 degrees. It slammed Irina right in the stomach and sent her flying over the side of the boat.

As she flew, she called out, "Robert!" Then she splashed into the churning water.

Robert didn't know what to do. He didn't dare let go of his daughter, but he had to help his wife. With one arm firmly gripping Athena, Robert crawled along the bottom of the boat until he reached an orange lifesaver clipped to the inside of the hull. He struggled to free it, and then crawled to the gunwale, fighting the storm for every inch.

"Irina! Grab this!"
He hurled the lifesaver with all his might. It flew towards Irina, but at the last moment the wind took it away. She couldn't reach the lifesaver, and she couldn't fight her way back to the boat.

As Robert knelt there, holding Athena with one hand and desperately clutching the railing with his other, he saw something he had never seen before: a giant whirlpool. It formed suddenly, spinning more than twenty feet across, and before Robert knew it Irina was in its grip. She was centered directly in the eye of the monster.

"Irina!"

-The Girl from Atlantis-

He looked around frantically for anything that might be of use. He pulled open a storage bench and yanked out several life jackets. He quickly strapped one onto Athena, and then hefted her into the storage unit.

"Don't move," he shouted. "Do you understand me?"

Athena nodded gravely.

"Just stay in here until I get you out."

"I promise, Daddy," Athena shouted over the wind.

Robert secured the hatch, and looked at the closed bench with grave misgivings. But she was safer in there than on deck, he reasoned. He hoped.

He strapped on the second life jacket, and pulled two more onto his left arm. Still fighting the wind, he climbed up the forestay, the wire cutting into his hands. He clutched the jib halyard, which was flapping loose.

"I'm coming!" he shouted, and leapt through the driving rain into the sea, as close to Irina as he could get.

He tried to grab her, but it was no use. The whirlpool was too wide, the current too strong, and the wind too fierce. He pulled one of the life jackets off his arm and stretched out towards Irina.

"Can you grab it?"

Irina kicked with all her might. She desperately reached for the life jacket, for Robert, for anything she could get her hands on, but she came up empty.

Robert tried throwing her the life jacket, but the wind took it far, far away. He yanked the second spare off his arm and once again reached out for her.

"Grab it!"

This time he tightly held onto one strap as he threw it towards her. She still couldn't reach, but at least he had hold of it.

Only now the whirlpool was pulling her down.

"No!" he yelled, the first time her face submerged.

He tried once more, and then again, to force himself into the eye of the churning water, to take hold of Irina or at least help her grab the life jacket. But each time he approached, the whirlpool thrust him away while it pulled her further down. He thought, *This is impossible… the thing has a mind of its own.*

In that instant, the wind blew the boat over. The mast crashed down, missing Robert's head by inches. Luckily the boat had blown towards him, so the storage bin where Athena was hiding was up out of the water. Robert looked back to Irina – the mast ran a few feet past her. And he realized he had a chance.

He scrambled up onto the mast, hooking both legs around it, and shimmied along the length of the long pole. As the boat rose up and down, he was pushed down into the water and then yanked up brutally, but he held on, and slowly approached Irina.

She was losing her battle with the whirlpool, her face bobbing up and down every second. She sputtered, "Robert…"
"Hold on, Irina. I'm coming!"

Finally, by superhuman effort, Robert was close enough to reach Irina. He struggled to hand her the life jacket and just as he did, he lost his balance, spun around completely and fell off the mast. He whirled around and around, drawn closer to the deadly eye where Irina was being pulled down.

Irina tried to put on the life jacket, but she was too far under water and spinning too fast to stay afloat.

Robert pushed his way across the raging waters, stretched out his arms to her, and just managed to touch her fingertips –

But at that instant, Irina was sucked down into the whirlpool.

And the moment she was gone – it all stopped. The whirlpool dissipated, the clouds parted, and it was a breezy, beautiful day once more.

Robert dove, again and again, into the deep blue water but he could find no trace of his wife. It was as though the sea had taken her by force and transported her far, far away in a matter of seconds.

Robert swam back to the boat and freed Athena from the storage bin. He radioed for help, and it arrived in just a few minutes. Divers scoured the area, but it was no use.

Robert led search parties for days afterwards, never sleeping and barely eating. He pushed his staff, along with every volunteer he could muster, into boats big and small. They searched above and below the water, both day and night, shining spotlights and calling Irina's name… but no trace of her was ever found.

# Chapter 6

At first, Athena didn't understand what had happened.

As much as she loved the sea, she knew that you couldn't spend all day in the ocean; you had to come out by dark and go home to bed. Her mother, however, didn't seem to be following that rule. It seemed like she just wanted to stay and stay in the water, and that wasn't really fair.

Robert patiently, sadly explained: "Sweetie, mommy is dead. Just like when redfish was lying in the bottom of his bowl. Just like when my grandma died before you were born."

Athena rejected that explanation. She shook her head so hard it hurt.
"Mommy wasn't old like your grandma, and she wasn't sick, either," she insisted.
Robert tried again, telling her, "There are other ways of dying. People have accidents. We were caught in a terrible storm."

Only three, Athena had a hard time finding the words with which to express herself. She understood they had been caught in a bad storm, but it didn't make sense that a person could go into the water and not come out again. People didn't *die* from *swimming*.

Robert explained about "drowning" over and over again; it just wouldn't stick.

"But Athena… you almost drowned. Remember? Don't you remember what it felt like when your lungs filled with water and you blacked out?"

She shook her head again. She simply didn't remember feeling any danger that day.

"Well, people can't live like that," Robert went on. "People need air in their lungs, not water. We can't go more than a few seconds without air or we die. And I'm afraid that's what happened to mommy."

"Then where is she? Even if she died, she's got to be somewhere." Athena had seen enough deceased fish, birds, and feral island cats to know that every dead animal left a body behind.

"I – I don't know. I looked everywhere for her, and I couldn't find her."

Well, that didn't make any sense at all. How could her father not be able to find her mother? That was his job – finding things underwater. He had found all sorts of secret, hidden things down there. How could he not find his own wife?

But when Athena put it like that –when she asked him about it just that way– Robert buried his face in his hands and cried. His shoulers shook up and down very hard, and tears streamed down his face. He cried like that boy Athena saw fall off the seesaw onto his head. He cried like Athena did when she cut her knee so badly one time that she needed stitches. He cried a way she'd never seen a grown up cry. And she decided right then that it was something she didn't want to see again.

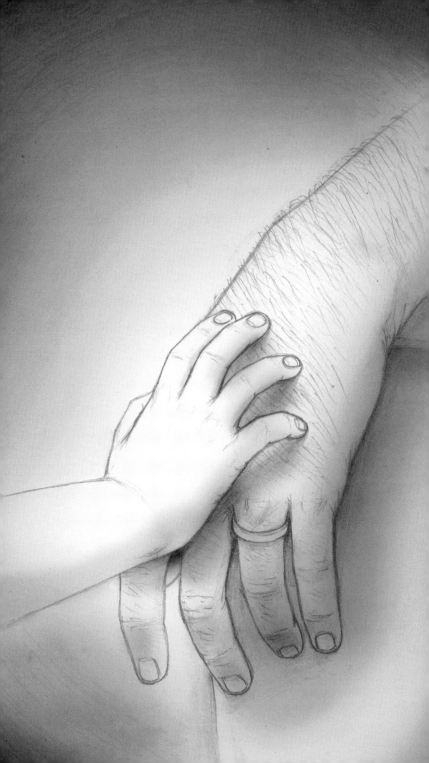

So Athena stopped asking about her mother, and Robert was quite relieved to not have to discuss the matter again. He locked away his sadness and concentrated on Athena. For her part, Athena eventually came to accept that her mother was gone, forever, and this was simply an adjustment she was going to have to make. Lots of kids had only one parent, and now she was one of them.

# Chapter 7

For a while, Robert considered leaving Atlantis and taking Athena home to California, where his family could help him raise her. But he was so dedicated to his work in the Bahamas, and Athena was so happy at Atlantis, that in the end he decided to stay. Even so, from then on he was very wary in small boats, and he always made sure that Athena wore a life preserver, even though she hated them.

Others at the resort chipped in to help Robert raise Athena. For example Sheridan, who ran the hotel "Kids Club", would babysit whenever Robert had to work late or travel off the island for a meeting. Sheridan was a young local woman who had proudly gone to The College of the Bahamas – the first in her family to do so. She was very sweet, and loved children. Athena thought Sheridan was the second-prettiest lady she had ever seen, with her smooth, dark brown skin and her sleek black hair rolling in neat waves down her back.

Athena loved hanging out in the Kids Club… there were books to read and games to play; there were arts and crafts projects; and there were children from all over the world with whom she could trade stories. She loved hearing about far away places like New York and London, and the young visitors were fascinated by a girl who could swim even before she could walk.

Another friend was Dexter, the "Blue Adventures" man. He was in charge of all the scuba and snorkeling boat trips. He was tall and thin, with coffee-colored skin, close-cropped hair and the whitest smile Athena had ever seen. And she saw it frequently, because Dexter was a funny young man who loved to laugh. He was always making small stones and shells appear from behind Athena's ears, or from between her toes, and he would accuse her of not bathing carefully enough. In turn, she would count his ribs, insisting that one had gone missing since the day before – and not incidentally causing him to howl in gales of ticklish laughter.

Dexter would often take Athena along on his trips. He taught her how to snorkel like a professional. She could do deep surface dives and hold her breath for a long, long time. She was handy to have along on dive trips because she could spot a stingray or a sea turtle while the tourists were still fumbling with their equipment. This was truly helpful since the visitors loved seeing the larger animals even more than they did the multitude of beautiful fish. And first time snorkelers always felt more comfortable around a small child who was so at ease in the water.

Athena had one strange problem in the ocean, however. She heard a terrible, painfully loud whine in her ears every time she was under the surface of the water.

Robert thought it might be an infection, and so he took Athena to the doctor. But there was nothing wrong in her ears. They even flew to Miami to visit a specialist, but she couldn't find anything physically wrong with Athena either.

The only solution they could come up with was a pair of swimmers' ear plugs.

These cut out the noise, but they also meant that Athena couldn't "clear" her nasal passages while diving deep… thus she couldn't learn to scuba dive. This made her sad, but it was only one more problem to overcome.

*     *     *

And when Athena turned five, there was school.

This took place in a little red schoolhouse on the far end of the island. It was built for the children of Paradise Island, as well as the families of some senior hotel staff. But many of those families only spent part of the year here, and most of the students were older than Athena. So while she excelled in her studies, she didn't build any lasting friendships.

Athena's life settled into a pleasantly predictable pattern. She spent her mornings at the small island school. In the afternoon she took a boat trip with Dexter, or went adventuring solo along a rocky stretch of shoreline, or tearing down the slides at the water park. Later she'd linger with Sheridan at the Kids Club.

Naturally, most evenings and weekends she spent with her father. They barbequed, swam, hiked, and read. She loved to curl up in Robert's lap while he read aloud from an old storybook, doing all the voices and making every page come magically to life. They read "Treasure Island" many, many times.

They didn't speak much of her mother. When Athena would ask too many questions about Irina, Robert would go quiet and his eyes would get watery. Athena hated seeing him so sad, so while she liked hearing stories about her mom, she rarely asked her father to tell any.

Athena kept a small album filled with photographs of Irina. Sometimes when she felt especially lonely she'd slowly flip through the pages, convincing herself she could actually remember experiencing the events in the pictures. And she always wore the little silver locket around her neck, with the baby picture of herself on one side, and the picture of Irina smiling on the other. In this way, she remained connected to her mother; long lost, but never forgotten.

# Chapter 8

As Athena got a little older, she was allowed to help out around Atlantis.

She volunteered at Dolphin Cay, the massive habitat created for 17 dolphins rescued when hurricane Katrina destroyed their original home in New Orleans. Athena's job was to hose down the fish buckets, and check the water tanks for debris. But of course she loved to watch the dolphins swim and play, chatter and tease.

And she had a remarkably strong rapport with the animals. She was sure she could even understand some of their jokes, but when she tried to repeat them, they never made any sense.

Athena also worked with the divers who maintained the tanks in The Dig, passing them equipment and helping to wash and organize their tools. The Dig was an aquarium where the hotel exhibited a stunning array of local sea life, as well as many of the ancient artifacts her father had recovered from the lost city of Atlantis. Athena felt especially proud whenever she worked in The Dig. Beautiful examples of her father's work were on display everywhere.

One day in The Dig, Athena was leaning against a big window in the Hall of Waters, gazing at a giant manta ray named Zeus.

She suddenly got the strongest sense that something was wrong. At first it was just a general feeling. But the more she concentrated, and the more she stared at the ray "flying" through the huge tank, the more she understood the problem.

Athena ran to find Maddie Miller, the manager of Marine Aquarium Operations at The Dig.

Maddie was in her office, turning off lights and getting ready to go home for the day. Athena was out of breath. "Maddie, Zeus isn't happy."

Maddie looked at Athena in just that way an adult will often look at a child when she's announced with certainty something the adult believes to be perfectly wrong.

Maddie sighed. "That's just his face, Athena. Manta rays always kind of look like they're frowning."

Athena shook her head. "No, that's not what I mean. He's happy enough, he's healthy – "
"I know he's healthy. We check him all the time." Maddie grew a little impatient.

Athena didn't quite know how to put it. She wasn't even sure *she* knew exactly what she was trying to say. After all, it had just been a feeling… But it was a *strong* feeling.

"He's feeling crowded. Maybe the tank is too small for him?"
"That tank holds nearly three million gallons of water!"
"Then maybe he's too big for the tank!"

Maddie took a sharp breath. She started to object, but stopped herself and thought a moment before speaking. At last she said, "No animal in captivity is ever going to have as much room as an animal in the wild, Athena... but Zeus *is* very big. And we've had him a long time. You know what? I'll look into it."

The next day Maddie and her team took some measurements and sure enough, Zeus' wingspan was almost 13 feet. He *was* getting too big for the tank, and he needed to be released.

And so began a huge adventure. First, a giant net strong enough to hold the 1000-pound animal but soft enough to not hurt his skin had to be hand woven. Next, special arrangements were made with the Association of Zoos and Aquariums to fit Zeus with a tag, so that international marine biologists would be able to track his movements once he was released. In this way they hoped to learn more about these rare and magnificent creatures (who are related to sharks, Athena learned).

Finally the day came. Twenty marine aquarists from Maddie's staff – plus Athena! – worked for over an hour to get Zeus into just the right position on the net. Athena kept whispering to him, telling him that everything was going to be okay if he could just be patient and stay calm.

Then a huge, powerful helicopter flew in and hovered over the tank while the net was attached to its underside. At the last moment, Athena patted Zeus' fin one final time and kissed him goodbye. It was the oddest thing, but she could have sworn she heard him say "goodbye... and thank you." Nobody else heard it, and in a moment she realized it was only her imagination.

At last, Zeus was lifted up by the helicopter and flown several miles out to sea, where divers were already waiting in the water to help him out of the net and on his way.

Everybody cried as he swam off into the deep ocean, but mostly they were tears of joy. They knew Zeus would be happier and ultimately healthier with a larger habitat to roam.

Later Maddie told Athena that Rose, a ray they had released several years before, was last tracked hundreds of miles away from Atlantis, off the coast of Georgia. Athena wondered if she'd ever see Zeus again… and decided that even if she didn't, she was happy she'd been able to help.

# Chapter 9

Athena was staring out the window of her fifth grade classroom one day when she realized that Time had a funny way of tricking people. It seemed to run at different speeds. For example, she thought, when you were sitting in a stuffy, quiet room, waiting to see a doctor, every second seemed to take a minute, or an hour, or… well, however long it was, nobody could wait that long.

But when you were fighting the waves in a perfectly warm ocean, or reading a thrilling story with your dad, the minutes just flew by until suddenly somebody was telling you that two hours had vanished and it was time to go in for supper. Just like that.

Since Athena's world was mostly perfect waves and thrilling stories, Time generally whooshed by like it was running for a train.

In this way several years passed, and suddenly Athena was 11-years-old. She was the sort of girl who had many adventures and accomplished quite a few things between the ages of five and eleven, but what happened over the next few days in Athena's life changed it forever.

\*       \*       \*

It began as a completely ordinary day. It rained much of the morning, but when school let out the sky was a cheery blue and a frisky breeze was dancing across the waves.

Athena was at one of her secret spots; a rocky promontory that nobody else liked to climb on because it was so full of sharp edges and small holes you could easily twist your ankle in. But Athena liked it. Sometimes, hidden in the pockets under just a little sand, you could find the most beautiful, unbroken shells anywhere on the island.

She was poking around the little pockets, some filled with salt water from the waves, and some filled with fresh water from the morning's rain, when something made her turn around. There, floating at the surface, just a few feet away, was the largest sea turtle she had ever seen.

He had kind, beautiful face, and Athena instantly knew this was a wise old turtle. His size was one indication of his age, but his eyes told her that he'd seen many creatures come and go over the years. She looked at him, and he seemed to be looking right at her.

She called out, "Hi, Mr. Turtle!"
He blinked at her, as if in response.

"How are you on this beautiful day?"
He cocked his head, opened his mouth… and quickly dove under the water.

"Well, nice talkin' to you!" Athena called out after him. She shook her head, smiling, and turned back to the water-pockets.

She reached her fingers deep into a hole and felt something smooth. She tried to pull it out, but it seemed stuck.

As she concentrated on pressing her fingers around the shell, she heard a deep, heavy breathing. She looked up, but there was no one there, so she turned her attention back to her efforts.

"It *is* a beautiful day..."

Startled, Athena looked up again. She saw no one, and yet she had definitely heard a voice, plain as day. It was a low, breathy voice, almost a whisper. She couldn't quite place the accent. She looked around again, saw no one, and decided that it had been her very active imagination.

And then she heard humming.

It was not a tune she recognized, but it was clearly the same voice which had spoken a moment ago.

She let go of the shell, stood up, and slowly looked all around. Indeed there was no one there except the turtle, which had returned. And… the turtle was humming. He rested one fin on the big rock where it submerged into the sea, and his head stuck out of the water. His mouth was opened slightly.

Athena sat down and looked directly at him. "Excuse me," she said.

The turtle did not look up, but he continued to hum.

"I might be losing my mind, but… I'm talking to you, Mr. Turtle. That was you who spoke, wasn't it?"

The turtle stopped humming, lifted his head, and faced Athena.

"You heard me, then? You understood?"

Athena was shocked. She hadn't actually expected the animal to answer her. She stammered for a moment, unsure of what to say.

"Well, I… yes. I suppose I did. Understand you."

"That's unusual."

"I'll say! You're a talking turtle!"

"All turtles speak, miss. There's nothing unusual about me. What's unusual is that you understood."

"Mr. Turtle, I – "

"Archibald."

"Arch – ?"

"Archibald. It's my name. What's yours?"

"Athena."

"Like the goddess?"

"Exactly. So, do I call you Archie?"

"Do I call you Athie?"

"No!"

"Well, then."

The turtle bowed his head a little bit.

"It's a pleasure to meet you, Athena. It's been a very, very long time since I conversed with a land-dweller."

"It's, um, nice to meet you, too."

Athena thought very hard for a few moments. What exactly did he mean, "All turtles speak?" Athena lived right next to an aquarium and she'd never heard of a single talking turtle.

"Mr. Archibald, sir. Maybe every turtle does speak. But none of them speak English. I'm sure *that* must be pretty rare."

Archibald blinked his eyes, and seemed to smile, although-turtles generally don't smile. They wheeze, they whisper, they click and grunt, moan and hiss, but they don't smile. Generally.

"I don't speak English. I speak Turtle. But because you can understand me, I suppose it sounds like English to you."

Athena lay down on the rock. This was way too much to think about on a Thursday afternoon. Now, somehow, all of a sudden, she could speak Turtle? Turtle that sounded like English? She sat up:

"How is it can I speak Turtle?"

"That's an excellent question. How can you?"

"No, it's not a quiz — I don't know. *I* was asking *you*."

"Hmm… Has anyone taught you?"

"No."

"Then it must be a natural ability. You must have been born with it. Have you spoken with any other animals?"

"No!"

"Never?"

Athena thought about it. She thought about the time at Dolphin Cay, when she somehow knew that Boomer, the young male, wanted to share a little tank time with Barbarella. She'd mentioned it to the keeper, who'd agreed to let the two be together. And then just a few weeks later Barbie was pregnant.

Then she thought about Zeus, and how she somehow knew he needed to get out of that tank. And she suddenly realized something very important:

"I can understand animals! Sometimes. Sea creatures, anyway."

"I see."

Archibald stuck his face in the water for a few seconds, and then came back up.

"Would you like to give it a try now, talking with some of my friends? There's a very chatty parrotfish and a fairly amusing grouper right down here."

Athena scrambled down the big rock and got on her hands and knees at the water's edge, next to Archibald. She took a deep breath and stuck her face in the water. She tried hard to listen, but all she heard was the familiar, noisy whine.

She pulled her head out of the water and shook the annoying sound out of her ears.

Archibald watched her expectantly.

"Well?"

"Sorry, Mr. Archibald. But every time I put my head under water, I hear this horrible noise. That's why I always wear ear plugs when I go snorkeling."

Archibald squinted at her, as though mildly annoyed, but this was only the face he made when he was thinking. He murmured, "I wonder what it is…"

Then his eyes went wide, and he nodded slowly.

Athena waited for further explanation.

Instead of offering any, Archibald asked, "Do you know the grotto under the big, flat rock? At the far end of the island?"

"Near the lighthouse?"

"That's it. Can you meet me there?"

"You mean, now?"

Archibald nodded. "I have a theory about your problem which I'd like to test."

Athena checked her watch. "Okay, but I can't stay out too late."

Athena's dad was attending a seminar in Mexico, and she was expected for dinner at the Kid's Club. It was a point of pride for her that she no longer needed a babysitter, but she had to eat, and she loved Sheridan. She pointed to her watch.

"How long will it take you to get there?"

There was Archibald's funny non-smile again. "I don't really measure the passage of time that way, Athena."

"Right. Well, I'll see you there."

She began to turn away… and then Archibald called out, "Bring your snorkeling mask."

He slipped under a small wave and was gone before she could respond.

# Chapter 10

The grotto was out at the far end of Paradise Island, where the island was so narrow you could nearly jump right across it. Just a thin strip of sand and brush, that's all it was. There was an old lighthouse that had warned boats to keep clear since 1817, and some debris left behind by teenagers who'd come out for picnics and campfires. It took Athena almost a half-hour to bike there. She pulled her snorkeling gear from her back pack and crawled inside the grotto.

It wasn't much of a grotto, really, but Athena loved it. The roof was created when a large, flat rock landed atop some small boulders. The rear wall was the result of hundreds of years of waves pounding the rock formation.

Her favorite part was the natural bench, a row of smooth rocks you could sit on with your legs in the water. The grotto wasn't quite tall enough to stand in, but several kids could sit comfortably on the bench and have a private conversation.

There was a great echo in the grotto, so it was easy to make scary voices, or to sound like a better singer than you really were. At high tide it was mostly under water, but mid-afternoon was low tide, so now the grotto was at its roomiest. There was about two feet of water sitting in the bottom, which was shaped like a giant soup spoon, due to the way the water had eroded the rock.

There were always a few fish swimming around in the bottom and Athena sometimes worried that they'd be trapped in the grotto when the tide went all the way out. But somehow they never were.

Athena checked her watch: 3:55 p.m. She wondered how long it would have taken the turtle to swim over from Shell Rock. Had he already been and gone? Or would she be waiting another hour for him?

She was not the sort of person prone to worrying; years of spending time alone had made her confident and self-reliant. But she really, really wanted to see this turtle again, and if he didn't show, she'd be so –

"Hello, Athena. I hope I haven't kept you waiting long."

There he was, his friendly old face sticking out of the water. She wanted to ask him about his voice – whether the breathy, wheezy quality was typical of all turtles, or if it was just because of his age – but she thought such a question could be thought rude.

"Nope, I just got here."
"Excellent. Now… I've brought some friends. I want to try an experiment."

Archibald stuck his head down into the bottom of the grotto. Some air bubbles came out of his mouth, and the fish that were swimming around all quickly left the grotto and went back into the ocean. Athena guessed that he had told them to leave.

"Now, please put your head under water and tell me if you hear anything."

Athena got on her knees, took a deep breath, closed her eyes, and stuck her head under water. It was quiet – almost as quiet as a pool! She didn't hear the awful noise.

"Well?"
"I didn't hear the sound."
"Good. Now, lean out over here, and put your head under again."

He wanted her to lean way out of the grotto and put her head into the open sea. She grabbed onto a rock in the side wall of the grotto, took a deep breath, and did as he instructed.

The moment her ears submerged, she heard the awful sound. She pulled up immediately.

"All right… I understand what's happening here," Archibald declared.

He motioned with his flipper, and a blue parrotfish swam back into the grotto.

"Athena, this is Percy. Please put on your mask now."

Athena quickly put on the snorkeling gear and dropped down into the water at the bottom of the grotto. Instead of darting away, Percy swam a little closer to Athena's face. He turned this way and that, opened his mouth, and spoke with a tiny little voice.

"Hello, Athena. Nice to meet you."

Athena couldn't talk because of the snorkel in her mouth but even if she could speak she still would have been staring silently, mouth agape. A little blue fish had just spoken to her.

She looked over at Archibald, who was also under water now, not-smiling at her.

Archibald motioned again with his flipper and several more parrotfish entered the grotto, along with a trunkfish, three yellow jacks, a cottonwick, and four, no – five porkfish.

"Hello."
"Hi, Athena."
"Hi there."
"Good afternoon."

They all started speaking at once and within a few moments it started to sound like that noise again… and suddenly Athena understood. She sat up and pulled off the mask excitedly.

"I can understand *every* sea creature! I hear them *all*, at once, whenever I go in the ocean! It's like a million people all yelling at me, all at the same time! *That's* the noise I hear whenever I go in the water!"

# Chapter 11

Athena rushed back and forth in the grotto, half crawling/
half swimming, clutching her diving mask, feeling like a
giant rock had just been lifted from her back. For as long
as she could remember, she'd wanted to know about that
noise, and now at last she did.

Archibald was looking at her, nodding. Athena wanted to
hug him.

"Thank you, Archibald. I don't know what to say!"
"But this is just the beginning, Athena."
"Of what?"
"My friends and I are going to teach you how to block out
the noise, and how to separate the voices from each other,
so that you can understand what is being said to you under
the sea."
"Wow. Really? Why?"
"Why not?"

*Sure. Why not?* Why shouldn't the talking turtle give her
lessons on how to speak with every creature in the sea?

In for a penny, in for a pound, as Dexter's mother sometimes
said.

"How do we start?"
"With Percy, I think, and the Carango triplets."

Archibald stuck his face in the water and in a moment only the parrot fish and the three yellow jacks remained. Athena put on her mask, went below, and waited silently.

"Hello, again."
This time she recognized Percy's voice, and nodded.

"Hi, Athena!"
It was the three yellow jacks, speaking as one. They sounded almost like children to Athena. She nodded at the silvery fish.

"We've seen you before. You're a fine swimmer."
Athena instinctively said, "Thank you," but since the snorkel was in her mouth it just came out as "blugh-bloo".

Archibald told them, "Now all of you speak at once."
Percy and the Carangos began to chatter. Because the yellow jacks spoke as one, it was pretty easy to tell them apart from the parrot fish. Archibald recited a poem, so now there were three voices going. Still, Athena could track what everyone was saying.

Archibald waved a fin and it was silent.
"You're doing well. Let's add a few more voices. Serra? Chaeto?"
A fat grouper swam in, followed by a few more small grouper, and a cute spotted butterfly fish. Archibald waited until they were in position, forming a semi-circle around Athena's head.
"Everyone?"

The fish all began speaking. It was a little like being in class just before the teacher comes in. Everyone is talking at the same time; it sounds like noise unless you focus in on just a few people, and then you can follow two or even three conversations at once.

Athena was surprised at how easy it was to sort out the voices, once you knew what you were listening to. She gave Archibald a thumbs-up and lifted her face out of the water.

As she pulled off her mask, he explained, "Just like land animals, sea creatures make all sorts of sounds. I daresay that many wouldn't even resemble voices to you. Perhaps this is why you found the undersea roar so unpleasant."

He left the grotto for a minute and came back with a sea star in his mouth. He placed the creature carefully on the stone floor.

"Try listening to this."
Athena put the mask back on and stuck her face near the star. She thought at first that it was moaning, but when she looked – and listened – more closely, she realized she was hearing was a whooshing sound, caused by water going in and out of its hundreds of tube feet. The sea star wasn't quite saying words, but Athena did get the sense it was communicating.
"I feel like it's greeting me, welcoming me to the neighborhood," she said.

Archibald nodded.
"The sea star doesn't have a brain, per se, and so it doesn't speak as you or I would. But like any creature with feelings, it can express itself. Oh! I think I hear a pod of dolphins coming by – "
"I've spoken with dolphins!"
"*Have* you?"

She explained about Boomer and Barbarella… and then told him about Zeus.
"So you suspected you could understand us."

"I felt something, but I didn't know what it was."
"Excellent. Well, let's get back to work…"

Over the next hour, all sorts of fish came and went. Snappers and hinds, chromis and grunts. Archibald coaxed in a crayfish and a nurse shark, and even a silvery barracuda came by briefly, but he stayed just outside the grotto. They came alone, in pairs, groups, and schools.

They spoke about all sorts of things; where they were from, where they'd been on their travels. They spoke of family; Athena told them about her father and his work, about how her mother had drowned when she was only three. The fish were particularly sympathetic to that story… many of them had seen their mothers pulled from the sea in nets or on hooks, even gobbled up by larger fish. But this was the nature of life, they observed.

Before long, Athena could identify most of their voices. She learned to pick out one or two creatures and focus her attention on them, ignoring the rest of the chatter. It was like sitting in a crowded baseball stadium; 26,000 people are talking at once, creating an enormous din, but you are conversing with the two people next to you without a problem.

It was a revelation.

The sun grew low in the sky, and Athena had to be getting home.
"Will you meet me here tomorrow, Archibald?"
"If you wish."
"Oh, I do wish! Thank you, Archibald. This is… amazing."

He sort of smiled one more time, sank into the water, and was gone. Athena scampered out of the grotto, dried off a little, and jumped on her bike.

She got home a bit late, and had missed a call from her father. When she phoned him back, he was in someone's presentation and had to speak in a whisper:

"Hey, sweetie. I can't really talk right now."
"I miss you, daddy!"
"I miss you too, darling. I'd call you later, but by the time I get out of this, it'll be way past your bedtime. Let's talk tomorrow, okay?"
"Okay! I love you!"
"I love you too, Athena."

She wanted to tell him about Archibald and all the rest of it, but it would be a long conversation she didn't want to have over the phone. Still, he'd be home Sunday night, and she could tell him then.

She made some notes in her journal about the afternoon's miraculous events, and that made her sleepy. She slept soundly, and dreamed all night of swimming through the ocean, laughing and joking with dozens of sea creature friends. It was a beautiful dream.

# Chapter 12

On Fridays, school sometimes let out early, and today was one of those times. *Hooray!* Athena hopped on her bike and tore out to the grotto as quickly as she could. She had a question she was burning to ask Archibald.

She practically threw herself into the grotto, but the turtle hadn't yet arrived. She thumped down onto the bench, frustrated. She watched two little redband parrotfish playing in the warm water. She suddenly jumped up, realizing that she could – *ooph!*

She hit her head on the grotto ceiling.

"Ouch," she yelled, rubbing her head. But she was too excited to stay grumpy. She pulled on her mask and knelt into the water.

She spoke directly to the fish.
"Hello! Hello there."

To Athena, her voice sounded mostly like humming and a lot of bubbles, but the parrotfish turned to face her.
"Hello," they said in unison.

"Do you happen to know Archibald, the sea turtle?"
The fish nodded.
"Would you please tell him that Athena is here to see him?"

The fish looked at each other, and then turned back to Athena.

"Okay."

And off they went.

While she waited, Athena leaned way out over the lip of the grotto floor, to see what she could pick out from the wall of sound that came at her. She was amazed that after only one day of practice the sound was no longer noise, but a sea of voices, and she was pleased she could pick out a few conversations.

She overheard an argument:

"That's not fair. *I* was going to eat him first. I was right there."

"I didn't see you, sorry."

"How could you not have seen me? I was *right there*."

"Look, if you were going to eat him, you should have just eaten him, instead of playing around that fan coral."

"So you *did* see me!"

She overheard a mother fish and her little fry:

"How many times have I told you? There's a reason it's red."

"But red is pretty."

"No. No. Red is *not* pretty. Red means 'stay away'. One of these days you're going to get too close, and I won't be there to…"

*Boy,* Athena thought. *All the creatures of the world really do have the same exact problems when it comes right down to it.*

She was concentrating on what she thought might have been two grey sharks in a philosophical debate when suddenly a deep, raspy voice said "Hello."

Athena looked over and Archibald was right next to her.

She sat up quickly and pulled off her mask.
"I'm so glad you're here," she said.
Archibald nodded respectfully, eyes crinkling with affection.
"I have to ask you something, Archibald. *Why* can I do this? Why me?"

He frowned, a much more natural expression for him than a smile, and narrowed his eyes. "I've been thinking about that. There aren't really a lot of possible reasons."
"What *are* the possible reasons?"
"Firstly… it could simply be some sort of one-of-a-kind accident of birth. A unique skill, like being able to read minds…"
"…or being able to compose a symphony at age six, like Mozart."
"Something like that, I suppose. It could also be that all of your kind can understand us, if they only take the time to listen."
"That's a nice idea, but I don't think so. The folks at Dolphin Cay would love to be able to talk to those animals, and they try all the time, but they never can."
"The other possibility is – what do you know about the undersea kingdom?"

Athena looked at Archibald and blinked.
"Nothing. I mean, I read 'The Little Mermaid'…"
"I think that perhaps… you may be a descendant of the Atlanteans."
"Atlanteans, like in, Atlantis?"
"Precisely."

Athena let out a low whistle. That was some coincidence.

"My father is the man who discovered the remains of Atlantis, right around here," she explained.

"Is that so?"

Athena nodded.

"He's a marine archaeologist. It's his job to go diving and look for relics of sunken ships, old civilizations, that sort of thing. He found the ruins of an ancient city, and everybody figured it was probably Atlantis. Or maybe they just wanted it to be, I don't know. But that's why the hotel is called 'Atlantis' and looks the way it does."

"Ah, yes. I know who he is. I've seen him at work over the years. I've always admired a certain… delicacy about his approach. He's very respectful of the environment. Frankly," Archibald said, seemingly revealing a secret, "if one of you people had to finally uncover Atlantis, I'm glad it was him. Someone who wouldn't make a mess of the whole place."

"Thanks!" Athena proudly said, "He made lots of other important discoveries, too. Although I guess none as big as Atlantis."

Archibald nodded thoughtfully. Athena sensed he knew something he wasn't saying.

"So how could I be a descendant of the Atlanteans?"

Archibald took a deep breath, and let it out slowly. He took another.

"Athena, the world is governed by rules. I imagine it's the same for land-dwellers as it is for those of us who live in the sea."

"Of course. My life is *full* of rules."

"I'm sure you can appreciate that there are consequences for those who break the rules."

"Oh, yeah. I get punished sometimes."

"Fine."

There was something he clearly did not want to say. But Athena had to know.

"Archibald, my father says that the city he discovered was destroyed at least three thousand years ago, probably longer. Which means that all the people who lived in it have been dead a long, long time. So... how could I be a descendant of theirs? And if I am, on what side of my family – my mother or my father?"

Archibald wasn't talking. *Why?* she thought. *Why is against the rules to talk about Atlantis?*

She worked on it in her head. The Atlanteans all died suddenly, three or more thousand years ago, but she was a descendant. How? And furthermore, they were simply people whose city was demolished in an earthquake. What did that have to do with talking to fish? It wasn't like the people who died in Pompeii learned how to walk on lava before they --

She sat up straight.
"They *didn't* all die. Some lived. Underwater somehow. There was something special about them and they adapted to life undersea."

Archibald bobbed his head vigorously, practically jumping up and down.

"Yes, yes! I wasn't allowed to tell you, but now you've figured it out for yourself. There were survivors, and their descendants are still living here, in an underwater city called Atlantica."

# Chapter 13

Athena had never heard anything so outrageous in her entire life. And she responded the only way she could: "No way, Archibald."

The sea turtle cocked his head.
"Do you think I'm lying to you?"
"No, no, of course not. But it's just impossible. I mean, an underwater city? How come we never discovered it?"
"They've learned a few tricks over the millennia about hiding from land-dwellers. And of course all the sea creatures are sworn to secrecy. Not that it's usually an issue. You people don't tend to ask us a lot of questions."

Athena screwed up her courage.
"Take me there!"

Archibald backed away from the girl.
"Oh, no. That's impossible."
"Why? You said yourself, I'm a descendant."
"It's not allowed. Triton would –"
"King Triton?"
"You know of him?"

"From, you know, stories. Cartoons. You're telling me he's real?"
"Oh, he's real."
"After all these years?"

"Yes. Well, no, even gods don't live forever… or sons of gods. No, this is Triton the twentieth, or twenty-fifth, or…

I don't know. I don't follow these things that closely. But the name and the title are handed down, father to son."
"What's he like?"
"They say he's fair man, but he's very powerful, with a temper to match. If I brought you-- "
"Just for a look. A tiny visit. We wouldn't even have to enter the city. Just peek at it, from outside."

Archibald frowned and instinctively shook his head back and forth.

"I have the right, Archibald. If some distant member of my family is from there, I deserve to at least see it."
"I don't know…"
"How far away is it?"
"Not very far at all. Sometimes I wonder that your people haven't found it."
"So just take me for a little look. We'll swim by, and come right back."

He did not respond. She gently placed a hand on his flipper.
"Please, Archibald. It would mean so much to me."
"I… I just…"
*"Please."*

Archibald pushed himself up on his flippers, gathering his resolve.
"Alright, then. But we'd better go now, before I change my mind."
"Great!"
"And just a peek."
"Absolutely."

Athena grabbed her mask and snorkel and put them on as Archibald maneuvered himself to begin their journey.
"Grab hold of my shell, just behind my flippers, and hold on tight."

Athena did as she was told. Archibald pushed off the bottom ledge of the grotto, and they were on their way. He was a fast, powerful swimmer, skimming just below the waves, while Athena breathed through her snorkel. As he swam, he spoke to Athena.

"I'm only about a hundred years old, so I can't say for sure how much of this is true. But this is the story as my mother told it to me."

He took a deep breath and continued. "Atlantis was no ordinary city. It was founded by a god. And not just any god, but Poseidon, master of the seas, and maker of earthquakes. He was the older brother of Zeus, who was god of the sky, and ruler of all the gods of the ancient world. Poseidon helped Zeus achieve that position by defeating their father for the throne, and Zeus rewarded Poseidon with a gift of the largest island in the ocean.

"Poseidon brought several wives to the island, both goddesses and humans, and they gave birth to many sons. The first he named Atlas. He named the city and then the entire ocean for this son.

"Poseidon himself lived in Atlantis for many years, until he finally returned to his sea palace near Greece. There, his wife Amphitrite gave birth to his son Triton, who was also a god, although not as strong as his father. But Poseidon did give Triton the powerful trident, and this has been passed down through the generations.

"The island city of Atlantis grew and prospered. The people were talented and handsome, and they became the finest race of land dwellers the world had ever seen. They sent magnificent ships to every corner of the world, trading goods and spreading wisdom and beauty.

It was said that every inventor, artist, philosopher, and poet anywhere in the world owed a debt to the Atlanteans.

"So they grew proud. And in their extreme pride they grew arrogant and decadent, and began to see themselves as gods among men. They made a dreadful mistake: they stopped worshipping Poseidon.

"It didn't take him long to find out, and it didn't take him long to act. He delivered a terrible earthquake to Atlantis, which destroyed the city and sent the island down to the bottom of the ocean, where it was covered in mud, and where it remained untouched until your father discovered pieces of it."

Athena muttered, "Wow," and in that moment realized something remarkable.

The entire time Archibald had been telling the story, he had been rapidly swimming along toward their destination. Athena was on his back, breathing through the snorkel.

But caught up in his tale and his goal, and perhaps a little distracted by the danger inherent in this quest, Archibald forgot that he needed to stay near the surface of the water. He'd descended deeper and deeper.

Spellbound by the story and the beautiful scenery flashing by her (because of her ears she had never been able to scuba dive before), Athena didn't notice the depth. Nor did she realize that even though they were 10, 20, 30 feet down in the ocean, she could still breathe.

But she realized it now, and started drowning.

# Chapter 14

Athena was choking, panicked, confused by her situation. Her brain was telling her, *You can't breathe under water!* but her body had been doing just fine until she became aware of it. To Athena, drowning was like being a cartoon character who steps off a cliff into thin air – but doesn't plummet until he remembers gravity.

Before death could take her, Archibald rushed her to the surface.
"Are you all right?"

Athena sputtered, coughing up water. She struggled to speak.
"How – how long were we down there?"
"I don't know – I'm so sorry!"
"No, it's okay… I'm – I'm fine. But how--"
"You were breathing under water."
"That's impossible!"

Archibald smiled, almost.
"And yet… it's true."

Athena had to admit, he was right. She definitely hadn't been holding her breath, and her lungs had been full of water. But she hadn't drowned. What on earth was going on here? What *was* she? She checked her legs – yep, still legs, so she wasn't some kind of mermaid. She could talk to animals, breathe under water… what *else* could she do?

Concern in his eyes, Archibald touched her with his flipper.
"Are you sure you're all right?"
"Absolutely. Let's keep going."
"No, that's not a good idea."
"But I can breathe underwater! I can!"

The first time, however, she'd done it by accident. This time she'd have to take in a lungful of water, fully conscious of what she was doing. That would be difficult, since up until this moment of her life, doing such a thing had pretty much meant drowning.

Athena looked at Archibald, still shaking his head. She spoke determinedly:
"When I was three years old, I almost drowned. That's what they told me, anyway. I fell out of a boat and went straight down, and when my father found me my lungs were full of water and I wasn't breathing. But Archibald... I was fine. And I remembered a big barracuda talking to me, telling me not to be afraid, and I wasn't. Everyone told me that I imagined the whole thing, and eventually I figured they were right. But now I understand... I'm an Atlantean. I can breathe underwater, I can talk to fish. I can do this. I don't know why, or how, but I can. Now I want to see Atlantica more than ever."

Archibald said, "Well, then. If you're ready..."
"Do you think... Maybe I don't need the mask?"
"I don't know. Take a look and see."

Athena pulled off her mask, and gazed into the water. At first, everything was blurry, just as it always was when she opened her eyes under water. But she blinked a few times, tried hard to focus on a long, dark reef, and sure enough, it became clear. She realized, however, that she was holding her breath.

She popped her face back above the water and took a big lungful of air.

"I don't need to wear the mask. Let's get going."

Archibald nodded. Athena stuck her arm through the strap of her face mask, grabbed hold of his shell, and he took off again.

He swam quickly, his powerful fins pushing through the water. At first Athena had a hard time keeping things in focus, but she quickly got the hang of it.

Again, she held her breath, dreading the terrifying moment when she would suck in a lungful of water. She held her breath for a good long time, but finally the moment came.

She gasped, opening her mouth wide, "breathing" in more water than she'd ever willingly taken into her mouth. For a long, horrible moment, she thought, *What have I done?* She felt she might black out... but she "breathed" the water back out – and she was fine. It seemed so strange that she did it again, right away, but the same thing happened.

She was sort of like a fish, she thought. Somehow, impossible as it seemed, her system could extract the oxygen she needed from the water she pulled into her lungs.

Calm now, she tried speaking: "Testing, one, two, three," she said. Her voice sounded different, because it was water, not air passing through her vocal chords. But she was speaking. She told Archibald, "I'm okay. I can breathe. But... how?"

He kept swimming as he spoke. "When Atlantis sank, not everyone drowned. Poseidon had all different kinds of children.

Humans, sea-creatures, gods and monsters. Those who could live underwater gathered together and built Atlantica, and Triton was sent to rule it.

"Some of the Atlanticans do look like you; they're basically land-dwellers who live under water. I imagine they're descended from Poseidon's half-human children. That must be why their ancestors survived the destruction of Atlantis. But most look like Triton; he's a – "
"A merman?"
"Yes. From the middle-up, he looks like a land-dweller. From the middle down, he looks like a sea creature."
"And it's mostly mer-people in Atlantica?"
"Oh, yes. They quite dominate. Indeed they…" He trailed off.
"What?"
"I don't live there, Athena. I wouldn't like to say."

Athena knew enough about the world to know what was on his mind.
"The mer-people look down on the humans, don't they?"
"It's just hearsay. I really wouldn't know."

They swam on in silence for a while after that. Athena enjoyed the scenery… there were beautiful reefs and dark caves; large grey sharks and all sorts of jellyfish; stingrays and eels; thousand and thousands of fish of every color. She saw creatures and reefs which don't exist near the surface. The deeper they went, the colder it grew, but that didn't bother Athena.

She was bothered more by the idea that she could swim into Atlantica and immediately be looked down on by some of its citizens. Athena had never looked down on anyone in her life, and she'd never allowed anyone to look down on her.

She had grown up surrounded by people of every color, who spoke all sorts of languages, from every corner of the world. She knew that you might judge a person by how they acted (especially toward animals!), but never by what they looked like.

And how could she be related to these people? Her father was from California; his grandparents had come to America as children, from Europe. Her mother was a local from the Bahamas, but she'd been an orphan, with no family at all...

As these thoughts ran through her head she noticed a massive coral reef with tendrils reaching up toward the surface. It was such an odd and giant formation...

She focused on it more closely, and realized – it was a castle.

Atlantica, dead ahead!

# Chapter 15

Archibald seemed to know what she was thinking. "Magnificent, isn't it?"

"It looks like a coral reef in the shape of a castle."

"Because it is."

Athena knew that corals are actually tiny, identical creatures that form colonies by the thousands. They create hard calcium skeletons which, over time, build one on top of another to create the beautiful corals and reefs you see in the ocean. But she'd never seen them build a castle.

"I don't understand," she said.

"Triton can command the creatures of the sea to do his bidding, from large to small," Archibald explained. "He simply ordered the corals to build it for him. His castle is essentially a made-to-order reef."

"Have you ever been inside?"

"A long time ago. It was a celebration for one of Triton's grand-children. It was very crowded, and I've never been comfortable in crowds. I only stayed a short while."

As they swam closer, Athena got a better sense of the city.

It was dominated by the castle, which was located in the center. The castle was hundreds of feet wide and about three stories high for the most part. There were three towers, however, which rose nearly 200 feet from the sea floor.

The rest of the city spread out from the castle in concentric circles.

The design of the buildings was similar to the reconstruction of Atlantis Robert Crowley had created from his findings. But there were smaller structures made of coral, and even items rescued from sunken ships. Athena saw what seemed to be a restaurant housed in the hull of a wrecked cruise liner.

The entire city was surrounded by a low wall which was primarily decorative. Athena wondered about that, and then had a sudden realization: *What's the point of having a higher wall? Any intruder could simply swim over it!* Athena looked up and saw a team of creatures she couldn't quite make out, circling the waters above the city in formation.

Archibald drew as close as he dared, and then swam in an arc around the city, giving Athena a better view. He stayed low, to keep out of sight of the guards.

"Can we go closer?" Athena asked.
"I'd better not. You shouldn't be seen."
"But I could blend right in."
"Not wearing that."
"What's wrong with my outfit?"

She was wearing a red and yellow one-piece bathing suit, cut-off jean shorts, and a tank top.
"They'll know in an instant that you're a land-dweller."
"I don't see how."

Archibald sighed, and swam closer to the city. The nearer they drew, the more visible the details became, and Athena could start to see the shapes of individuals moving from place to place.

Now she could see that while the narrow circular paths had the appearance of "roads," there were no vehicles moving along them; only mer-people swimming one way or the other.

Athena squinted to get a better look at the people. In her wildest imagination, she never pictured anything like it… an entire city of mermaids and mermen! Hundreds of them, heading this way and that.

As for their dress – the mer-people weren't really wearing anything at all! A few had on necklaces, or other adornments around their waist, wrist, or head, but other than that, they were completely nude. For the most part, they looked like the mermaids and mermen she'd seen in paintings and cartoons, but with one big difference: their tales weren't scaly.

She was going to ask Archibald about this when it occurred to her that their tales should not be scaly at all. Why would they be? These creatures were mammals, just like she was, or like a whale, a dolphin, or seal. They weren't fish, and therefore wouldn't have scales. They were, however, the most beautiful people Athena had ever seen, with lovely features and long hair flowing behind them as they swam through the city.

She looked for people like herself; there were none.

 "We need to get closer, Archibald. I don't see any… people like me."
"I don't think it's a good idea."
"Please, Archibald. I just want to see."
"I'm sure no good can come of this."
"I'll be careful, I promise."

Archibald swam down to the ocean floor, away from the main entrance to the city, and away from the guards circling high overhead. Athena swam to the wall and peered over. There were fish darting to and fro, and mer-people talking and laughing as they went on their way, but no humans. She turned back to Archibald and called out, "I'll be right back!"

Before Archibald could even whisper, "No!" she slipped over the wall and swam along a street. She passed a few small houses and decided to stop and take a look inside one.

She found a round window, about two feet across. There was no glass – what would have been the point? – and she could see right in. The furnishings reminded her of the Atlantean artifacts on display in The Dig. It was all very simple; something that seemed like a sofa, a few bulky items which were probably chairs. There didn't seem to be anyone home, so she leaned in just a little bit farther and –

"What do you think you're doing?"

Athena felt a strong hand grip her shoulder and yank her straight back. She turned around and found herself under the powerful gaze of a massive merman with a broad chest and muscular arms. The hand that gripped her was very strong, and there was webbing between his fingers. He had long black hair, a long straight nose, and a square chin. And dark, angry eyes.

# Chapter 16

"**W**ell? What are you doing, spying on a Citizen."

Athena knew she hadn't done anything wrong. If she could just explain herself –
"Answer me, biped!" shouted the merman.
"I'm not a biped!"

The merman's grip loosened slightly, taken aback as he was by her response. Of course she was a biped; the word simply meant that she had two legs. But in her agitated state, Athena had forgotten this.

The merman asked, "Wha- what do you mean?"
"I'm… a visitor. I just arrived in the city. From… from out of town."

Athena looked over her shoulder to see if Archibald was watching. He seemed to be gone. The merman followed her gaze, and he saw nothing as well. Archibald had simply ducked down behind the low wall, but Athena didn't know this. Suddenly the merman tightened his grip on her shoulder again.
"I think you're just a thief looking for her next victim."
"No! That's not true. I'm not a thief."
"You can tell that to the magistrate. Come along."

And before Athena could say or do anything, the merman pulled her along with him. He was far too powerful to resist.

Maybe if she explained her situation to someone in authority, she thought, they'd let her go. After all, she was just a kid.

As the merman whisked her through the streets of the city, Athena felt the disapproving looks of everyone they passed. Mermaids chatting with friends gasped slightly before leaning in close to each other and whispering animatedly. Mermen engaged in friendly banter grew dark and serious as they passed. And everyone looked at Athena as if she were some kind of animal – a pest, a rodent, evidence of an infestation.

Athena realized she was being brought to the castle. *Good,* she thought. *Maybe I'll get to see Triton. Archibald said he's fair.* She saw the grand gates at the main entrance… they seemed welcoming. However the merman jerked her along and brought her to a side entrance. He stopped in front of another large merman wearing an official-looking arm-band. Athena realized he must be some sort of policeman.

The first merman said rather proudly, "I caught this one peering into a citizen's home. I think she was planning a theft."
The police merman wearing the arm-band peered at Athena suspiciously. "Where are you supposed to be right now?"
Athena was frightened, but she knew she hadn't done anything wrong. "Nowhere. I'm just visiting."

This startled the policeman a bit. Biped humans didn't just turn up in Atlantica. "Visiting? From where?"
"From… Atlantis."
The policeman knew perfectly well that Atlantis had been destroyed thousands of years ago. He frowned at her, "What's that supposed to mean?"

"I live in Atlantis. The one…" She pointed up. The two mermen instinctively looked up. It slowly dawned on them what she was saying. The merman who had initially grabbed her slowly backed away. He wanted no part of this girl. What was a land-dweller doing in Atlantica?

The policeman said, "You'd better come with me." He grabbed Athena firmly by the arm and pulled her deeper into the station.

They passed a small, barred cell in which a number of suspects were being held. There was a shark angrily swimming back and forth, and in the corner there was a sea turtle! Athena peered as closely as she could at the turtle… and was relieved to see it was not Archibald.

There were several people in the cell who looked like her, except for their dress. They had simple caftans, or ponchos, covering themselves. These appeared to be woven from kelp, or some other kind of long, stringy seaweed. The garments provided only a basic cover for modesty; they clearly weren't intended to give any protection from the elements.

At first Athena thought she would be thrown into the cell, but the policeman dragged her along to where a supervisor of some sort sat in a large chair.

"Sir…?"
The supervisor looked up. He was an older merman, with features not as handsome as most of the others. He was heavier, as though he spent most of his time sitting, rather than swimming. His skin was an unattractive grey, and his hair was mostly gone. Without changing his expression, he grunted, "Hmm?"

"Sir, this young biped was brought in, caught spying on a citizen. She claims to be from the surface."

The supervisor's eyes widened and the corners of his mouth turned down. He turned his gaze from the policeman to Athena, carefully eyeing her hair and dress. When he spoke, his voice was deep, rough, and gravelly, as though rarely used.

"Is it true? Are you from the surface? Or did you simply find those clothes in a wreck and steal them from a drowned human child?"

# Chapter 17

Athena couldn't believe her ears. Put on clothes she found in a wreck?

She sputtered, "Gross! Why would I do that?"

The supervisor's mouth turned into a half-grimace, which on his face passed for a smile.

"Feel above your station, do you? Perhaps ready to try your luck among the land dwellers?"

A low rumble echoed from his center, which Athena took to be his laugh. The policeman who held her arm laughed, too. "Think you're the first? You bipeds all believe life is better on the surface… you don't know how good you have it here."

"I don't know anything about life here. I was born and raised on Paradise Island. You can ask the turtle who-"

"Enough!" The supervisor didn't rise, but he did seem to get bigger. "If your parents cannot be located, you'll be placed into service at the king's discretion. In the meantime, we'll hold you here. What's your name?"

"Athena Crowley. I'm 11 years-old."

"Crowley, you say?"

Athena nodded. "C, r, o, w, l, e, y. Crowley. My father is Robert."

The supervisor frowned more deeply than before. "You're lying. I've never heard that name before. there are any families here called 'Crowley'."

"He wasn't born here, like I told you. He's from Cali-"
"Silence!" He turned to a uniformed clerk. "Go to the records room and look it up, will you?"

He nodded ever so slightly to the policeman, who dragged Athena over to the barred cell. He unlocked it, and thrust her inside. At first, the others avoided looking at her. The people scooted over a little bit so that she could sit down. But she didn't want to sit down. She was angry.

"What's going on here? Why won't these guys believe me?"
The others were reluctant to respond. Athena looked around the tiny cell. There was an older woman, with gray hair and a face that showed a lifetime of despair. Next was a couple, who appeared to Athena to be in their mid-thirties. And there was a bald man with scars all over his face and arms. The shark glared at her and turned away. The turtle retreated further into the corner.

The younger woman indicated that Athena should sit down. Athena shook her head and ground her teeth.
"Please?" The woman had a gentle voice.

Harumphing, Athena sat next to her on the bench and angrily folded her arms across her chest. The woman turned to Athena and spoke quietly.
"Are you really from the surface?"
Athena nodded.
"Why did you come here?"
"A friend said I probably have family here… because I can – because of how I am. Like you."
"Who are your parents?"
"My father is a scientist, Robert Crowley, like I told him." She angrily tossed her head in the direction of the supervisor. "And my mother is dead."

The woman nodded sympathetically. "What was her name?"

"Irina."

"That's a beautiful name. I know several women named Irina and they are all lovely and kind."

"I don't remember her very well, but she was definitely lovely and – "

"Watch where you're going!"

The voice came from the bald, scarred man, who was standing, poised threateningly, glowering at the shark.

The shark had a raspy voice, higher-pitched than Athena would have suspected.

"It was an accident… this is a small space."

"I don't see anybody else smacking me in the face."

In a flash, the shark whipped around and was nose-to-nose with the man.

"I'm a large fish, and this is a small cell. It was an accident. Or do you want it to be a problem?"

"I'm ready when you are. You think I'm afraid of you? I'll add your teeth to my collection."

Athena noticed now that indeed the man wore a necklace with dozens of shark teeth. And she realized how he had gotten all those scars.

Suddenly the old woman stood up. "Would you two calm down? Look where you are! You're already *in* jail. Do you really want to make this worse?"

The shark half-turned towards her. "Can it get any worse?"

"It can always get worse. Believe me…"

The tension held for a few seconds longer… and then the shark backed slowly away from the man.

While it continued to "pace" back and forth, it did its best to avoid him. The man sat down, grumbling.

With the situation back to normal, Athena turned again to the younger woman.
"Why are you in here?"
"My husband and I tried to leave the city but the guards stopped us."
"Why would you want to leave? This city is beautiful."
The woman looked at her husband, and smiled ruefully. She looked at Athena and shook her head. "You really aren't from here, are you?"
Athena said, "No."

The woman took Athena's hand and held it tightly.
"Then you don't know what it's like to live your life as a slave."

# Chapter 18

Athena's eyes went wide and her jaw dropped open. Slaves! In this day and age?

As if reading Athena's thoughts, the woman nodded and said, "Yes. That's how they treat us. They always have. From the king on down to the lowliest guard. The mer-people are the 'citizens' and we…"

Her husband spoke up.

"We do all the work. We prepare their food, we clean up after them. We build their homes, we watch their young."

Athena was confused. "But you get paid, right?"

The husband smirked. "We're given a place to live, and food to eat. Occasionally they toss us a few coins. We make our own clothing and care for ourselves." His voice started to rise. "We're as good as they are, as smart, as capable, and yet we are kept – "

"Shhhhh…" His wife attempted to calm him.

The old woman leaned in. "It's best not to speak of these things. This is how it's always been, and how it will always be. The natural order of things."

The young husband scoffed at the woman. "Things can change. The world changes. Species come and go. The ocean gets warmer and everything is altered. So why can't this change?"

The woman shrugged and shook her head, as if to say, *I don't know why, but it won't.*

-The Girl from Atlantis-

Athena asked the old woman, "So why are you here?"

The woman straightened her back and answered, "My grand-daughter was playing in the path, and she inadvertently blocked a citizen for a moment. He could have just gone on his way, but he spoke rudely to her. I was too proud, and I answered back. A magistrate heard me and… here I am."
She looked at Athena, but she was speaking to the young husband. "It is important to know your place."
Athena nodded. "Well, my place is at home with my dad…"

She realized, "Oh, no, my dad! If I'm not home tonight when he calls, he'll be worried sick! I've got to get out of here!"

She jumped up and pressed her face between the bars of the cell. "*Hey!* Hey, I gotta get out of here!"
At first the policemen ignored her.
"Hey! I gotta go home!"
A gruff voice called out, "Be quiet."
"You don't understand. If I'm not home tonight, my father's gonna freak out. He'll think something really bad happened to me."

The moment the words were out of her mouth, she realized their foolishness. She was in jail, hundreds of feet below the surface of the sea. Something pretty bad had *already* happened to her!

While she was pondering that, the clerk and the policeman approached the cell. Even by merman standards, the clerk was what the kids in Athena's school would have called a "nerd." He didn't wear glasses, but he lacked the beautiful, flowing hair the others had, and his skin was mottled and colorless.

He spoke in a thin, reedy voice. "Despite your claims, there is no record of a Robert Crowley or an Athena Crowley in the records of Atlantica. Therefore, there is no way to establish lineage. Therefore, you will be immediately transferred to the care of the Royal Foundling Service, who will find suitable work and housing for you. Officer?"

The policeman unlocked the cell and roughly pulled Athena out. As he was closing the door, the bald man made a move to escape – but as he tried to squeeze through the door opening, the officer turned quickly and punched the man in the face. He fell backwards, his nose bleeding. The blood swirled in a small cloud around his head; the shark smelled it and immediately perked up, swimming back and forth in a more agitated state.

Athena never learned what happened next because she was dragged away. He yanked her down a long hallway, through a series of doors, and then another long hallway, all apparently underground. She and the policeman approached a sentry, who waved them through a checkpoint, and she realized that she was in the castle proper. The floors were polished, and the walls were decorated with beautiful carvings of mer-people and other sea creatures.

She tried to take it all in, but the policeman kept pulling her along. The hallway narrowed, and they approached a closed door with a number of Atlantean characters carved on it. Athena had not yet learned much of the Atlantean language her father discovered, but she knew enough to read the word "Royal" on the door. She determined that wherever they were going, they'd arrived.

The policeman opened the door and there, sitting at a desk, was a fat old mermaid.

To Athena, she looked almost like a manatee! As they stepped farther into the room, the mermaid looked up: "Yes?"

"Got a foundling for you. No family, no home."

The aging mermaid smiled at Athena. "What's your name, dear?"

Athena told her.

"And where are you from?"

The officer spoke up. "She claims to be from the surface."

"I *am* from the surface!"

The mermaid rose and cleared her throat. "No matter where you're *from*, dear, this is your home now. We'll take care of you. Welcome to the royal castle!"

Athena understood that this 'warm welcome' was supposed to make her feel better, and at least this woman seemed nicer than the police had been. But all she knew was that she was being taken further away from her father and her home.

# Chapter 19

Back on land, Robert Crowley was on a break between the last panel of the day, "Archeological Conservation using Polymers in Ixtapa," and dinner. He made his way to a quiet corner and pulled out his cell phone.

He dialed his home, and frowned when the answering machine picked up. He called out, hoping someone would hear him. "Hello, hello? Anybody home? Athena? Athena, it's daddy!"

No one picked up. He checked the time again, mentally added two hours, and frowned once more. She should be home by now. He dialed Sheridan's cell phone; she picked up after two rings.

"It's another beautiful day in the Bahamas, Sheridan speaking!"

"Sheridan, it's me, Robert Crowley."

"Oh, good evening, Dr. Robert. How is your trip?"

"It's fine Sheridan. Look, is Athena with you?"

"No, sir. I haven't seen her all day."

"Any idea where she is?"

"She's not at home?"

"She didn't answer the phone."

"She could be in the shower. Maybe using headphones, something like that."

Robert nodded, "That's true. Well, if you see her, please have her call me. I'll be at dinner, but it doesn't matter. I want to speak with her."

"Absolutely, Dr. Robert."

And she added, "Don't worry about Athena. She's a good girl. She won't get herself into any trouble."

"I know. I just... I just miss her, that's all. Thanks!"

Robert clicked off the phone. He knew he shouldn't worry about Athena... but he did anyway. It just didn't feel right somehow, not speaking to her all day.

*　　　*　　　*

Archibald wasn't sure exactly how long he'd been lying motionless on the sea floor, but he decided it was long enough. He slowly rose up and poked his nose over the low wall, scanning for any sign of Athena or the angry merman. They were, as he suspected, long gone.

He was an old turtle and so he moved through emotions slowly. Sitting there in the shadow of the wall, he gradually grew angry at Athena for ignoring his warnings and entering the city. *What a willful child,* he thought. *Why not listen to reason?* The longer he pondered these feelings, however, the more forgiving he became and the calmer he grew, only to feel anger rise once more – this time aimed at himself. *What a fool I was to have told her about Atlantica! To have brought her here! To have allowed her to leave my side!*

He cursed himself a coward for allowing the merman to take her away... and then reminded himself that he would have been powerless to stop it. And if he'd been captured as well, then Athena would be trapped forever with no chance of getting home.

So that was now his mission: to locate Athena, and pilot her escape, because no good could come of her continued presence in Atlantica.

# Chapter 20

The aged mermaid was named Melora, and she'd run the King's foundling program for many, many years. She saw herself as a motherly influence on all the poor unfortunates who came under her care. Melora had raised several generations of orphans, and was proud of the hard workers they had become.

She simply had no idea that the young humans in her care looked upon her with anything other than affection.

She guided Athena to the dormitory where the foundlings lived. It seemed to Athena more like a prison than a dorm, but then she'd never been to college and so she didn't know for sure. Just before they entered, Athena heard a loud gong; not quite a bell ringing – more like a metal rod clanging against a hollow pipe. The sound of it carried sharply through the water.

Suddenly there was a tremendous hustle and bustle in the hallway. Boys and girls, ranging in age from five or six up to young teenagers, were flying out of the little dorm rooms and rushing on their way. All were careful to avoid bumping into Melora or to even make eye contact. Still, she smiled benevolently at everyone, calling out, "Hurry, darlings! Don't be late for your work shift!"

She turned to Athena and explained that it was time for the night-shift to begin.

-The Girl from Atlantis-

Running the castle was a night and day operation. The children who'd been working all day would finally get some rest, taking the place of those who'd been sleeping until just a few moments ago. Each child shared a bed with another. "Why bother having a bed sit empty all day? That's just wasteful," Melora cheerfully observed.

Down the hall an argument grew louder. Melora took Athena's hand and moved her along. As they approached, she called out, "What's this?"

A tired and angry girl about Athena's age was standing in a doorway, on the verge of tears. "She won't get up. She won't get up and go to work. I need to lie down. I'm exhausted."

Melora peered into the tiny bedroom. "Well?"
Curled up on the bed was a pale, sickly girl. "I don't feel well. I need more sleep."
"Rest time is over, dear. It's time to go to work."
"I can't tonight… let me sleep."
"Then where is poor – " She raised an eyebrow at the angry girl, as if to say, *What's your name?*
"Nettie."
"Where is poor Nettie to sleep if you stay in bed?"
The sick girl buried her face on the mat. "I don't care."
Melora frowned. "That's no attitude to have. Come out of there at once."
This was met with silence.

Melora somehow changed before Athena's eyes. Her expression grew fierce, and she seemed to get bigger. Athena could have sworn her eyes glowed red. Melora's voice became a furious growl: "Get out of that room now, or you'll never feel the comfort of a bed again."

The sick girl got up at once and fled the room. Nettie nodded at Melora, and slipped into the bed as quickly as she could.

In the time it took for that exchange to happen, Melora assumed her previous appearance and friendly tone. "I'm so pleased we settled *that*. Now… "
She scanned the hallway, and then pointed. "That'll be your room, number 24. But before we put you in a room, let's find you a job!"

Athena thought a rest would do her some good, however she already knew better than to contradict Melora.

The mermaid jerked her along in the crush of young workers scurrying to their posts. They went down a passageway and along another long hallway, ending in the castle's vast kitchen.

Athena wondered how they might cook under the sea, since you couldn't exactly light a fire, and now she saw the answer. The stoves and ovens were heated by geothermal vents!

These were naturally occurring fissures in the ocean floor that looked like stalagmites (those cone-shaped formations you might see in a cave). Deep underground, water was super-heated, either by volcanic activity or another kind of chemical reaction. Where the water shot up and emerged from these vents, the mer-people had built stoves and ovens to capture the heat. Athena reasoned that these vents might have been the reason Atlantica was built here in the first place.

Athena recognized several of the pots and pans because they were identical to artifacts her father discovered.

In fact, he'd never been able to figure out what some of these items were for; Athena couldn't wait to tell him they were cookware!

Her father… Athena realized that he must have called by now, and was probably pretty upset he hadn't reached her. *Well, maybe he's so busy in Mexico he didn't even notice I'm not around*, she thought … *Fat chance.*

Melora saw Athena staring at the cooking stations. "You must never touch any of that. It's all very hot and if you burn yourself, you won't be able to work, will you?" She looked around. "No, I think we'll start you off with something nice and simple. Dishwashing!"

She walked Athena to the next room, where a half-dozen women were standing around a circular table piled high with dishes, glasses, pots, and pans. She couldn't quite see what was in the center of the circle, until she got closer and realized it was – incredibly – a whirlpool, about four feet across, hovering directly over a similarly sized hole in the ocean floor.

The women and girls were taking the dirty dishes and, while keeping a firm grip on each item, placing them into the spinning vortex of the whirlpool. The action of the water cleaned off any residue, and the debris flowed through the swirling center of the whirlpool until it disappeared down the hole. It was one of the most amazing things Athena had ever seen.

Melora casually tossed her head in the direction of the dishwashing station. "I believe the method is self-evident. If you have any questions, ask Irina. She's been here the longest."

*Irina… that was her mother's name.*

Athena wondered, was it good or bad that the chief dishwasher's name was so familiar? Would it bring comfort, ease this transition into slave labor until she could figure out how to escape? Or would it be a constant torment, a reminder of what she had lost?

Melora turned and left, and while Athena was still pondering these questions she moved over to the dishwashing table. She examined the faces of the women, looking for the eldest, trying to identify "Irina."

Athena stopped in her tracks. She stopped breathing. She believed her heart stopped beating for a moment.

Because the woman she was staring at looked *exactly* like her own mother!

# Chapter 21

Athena could not find words, so she just stood there, staring. This woman was certainly older, more weathered-looking than the person in Athena's photo album. Her eyes didn't sparkle with life, as her mother's had. And she didn't appear to smile. But she was otherwise her mother's twin.

Soon one, then another, then all the girls and women were looking back at Athena, most of them smiling, amused by the young girl staring intently, eyes fixed on Irina.

The first one to speak was Aithra, a black-haired girl a few years older than Athena. She had big, brown eyes and a friendly smile. "First day?" she asked.
Athena managed to nod.
"Don't be scared. It's not so bad. The shift goes by and then you rest. C'mon, I'll show you how it's done…"

She moved over, making a place for Athena at the table. Athena slowly glided over. Aithra picked up a plate, holding it firmly by the edge. She placed it about ¾ of the way into the whirlpool, and in an instant, it was nearly clean. She switched hands, reversed the process, and it was done. She added the plate to a pile of clean dishes on a cart directly behind her. "See? Easy. You try."

Still staring at Irina, Athena picked up a plate and held it unsteadily over the whirlpool. She started to dip it in…

and the spinning current whipped the plate out of her hand, rotating it round and round and downward, pulling it into the hole in the ground. The plate vanished entirely in an instant.

The others laughed good-naturedly. Tyro, a heavy-set woman in her twenties, spoke up. "Don't worry! Everybody does it at first… just don't ever let Melora see you drop a plate or she'll dock a meal!"

Athena mumbled, "Okay…thanks."

Tyro continued, "So, what's your name?"

"Athena." Athena watched Irina's face for some sign of recognition…or at least interest. But she merely continued her work with a blank expression on her face.

"Nice to meet you. I'm Tyro. That's Aithra, Erinys, Amymone –

"Call me 'Amy.'"

"—Lucina, and Irina, in whom you already seem to have an interest."

Athena managed a smile. "Nice to meet all of you."

The others nodded and murmured pleasantries, and then continued with their work. But Athena could not concentrate. This woman was *so like* her mother…

As a teenage boy arrived with a large tray full of dirty dishes, Athena murmured, "Irina?"

The woman looked up, still half in a daze. "Hmm?"

"Do I… do you recognize me at all?"

Irina squinted at Athena, as though not quite understanding the question.

"Do I look familiar to you? Because you look really familiar to me."

Irina considered the question. "I'm sorry, no. What's your name again?"

"Athena."

"Athena… hmm." She struggled to remember. Was that a flicker of a memory in her eyes? "No, sorry, dear. I don't think so." She gave a little half-smile and went back to work.

Tyro leaned in close to Athena and whispered, "You have to forgive Irina. She had a little trouble a few years back."
"What happened?"
"I'll tell you later."

Frustrated, Athena picked up a dirty plate and, holding it much more firmly, dipped it into the whirlpool. The force of the spinning current pulled at the plate, but she held on tight. She managed to change hands without letting it slip, and then it was done. She'd washed her first plate as a slave of King Triton's. A dubious achievement, she decided.

They continued to work in silence.

\*       \*       \*

Robert Crowley was beside himself with worry. It was now late at night in the Bahamas, and there was still no word from Athena. He'd left numerous messages on their machine, and he'd called Sheridan and Dexter repeatedly. He'd telephoned several other friends and co-workers but no one had seen Athena, nor had any idea where she might be. Hard as he tried, Robert couldn't stop himself from imagining the worst. What if she'd gone swimming alone? Or on a small boat? Something could have happened…

He shook his head. No. Athena knew better than that. She'd never go alone on a boat. She'd never go swimming in dangerous waters. And if she was going to go adventuring, she'd tell someone about it.

*She's probably just having a sleepover with a friend and forgot to leave word.* He instinctively checked his cell phone again for messages – none. Maybe Sheridan was right earlier. Maybe Athena was just asleep with headphones on and never heard the phone. There were so many possible explanations; he was crazy to worry this much. Even the police told him they needed to wait until Athena had been missing for twenty-four hours before they could get involved.

And yet…

He dialed the number of Mrs. Lucy, their elderly neighbor. There'd been no answer earlier, but maybe now –
"Hello?"
"Mrs. Lucy? It's Robert Crowley."
"Oh, hello, Dr. Robert. Where are you? You sound far away."
"I'm in Mexico, at a scientific conference. Say, Mrs. Lucy, do you still have the emergency key I gave you?"
"Key?"
"To my house."
"Oh, yes. I'm sure I have it here somewhere…"
She put down the phone and started searching her kitchen drawers for the key. Robert could hear her singing to herself as she slowly slid drawers open and closed, fishing around among the screws and nuts, spare bits of this and that and miscellaneous junk most people keep in their kitchen drawers. The wait was interminable. He muttered to himself, "C'mon-c'mon-c'mon-c'mon-c'mon…"

Finally she picked up the receiver.
"A brass key or a silver key?"
"Brass."
"Oh, dear…wait - I think I have it right here. Do you need it?"

"No, Mrs. Lucy. I was hoping you could go into my house and check on Athena."

"Now?"

"If you wouldn't mind. I know it's late, I'm sorry."

"No, no, it's no problem…"

She put the phone down on the counter, and shuffled out of the room.

Robert lay back on his hotel room bed, clutching the phone, sweating with concern. His next call would be to the airline.

# Chapter 22

Archibald was growing tired. For hours – he wasn't sure how many – he'd been circling Atlantica, looking for any trace of Athena. And now it was getting quite dark.

He'd learned more about the city in the last few hours than he had in years. He simply never paid such close attention before. He knew now that the castle was truly the center of Atlantican life. Mer-people came and went constantly, and more of them went to and came from the castle than any other single location. The bustle of activity led him to believe an event might be happening soon.

He also observed a shift-change, and noticed that not all the guards attending the many gates to the city were particularly dedicated to their job. For every replacement guard who turned up at his post a few minutes early, there was another who arrived a few moments late. He filed this away as potentially useful information.

Archibald pictured people coming and going through gates, holding flags above their heads, marching in time to music… Suddenly he shook his head and forced his eyes open wide. He'd been drifting off to sleep, and that was something he could not do. He had to find Athena, and determine a method of rescue.

But he was so tired…

\*        \*        \*

Aithra had been correct; the time did fly by. They worked through the initial piles of dishes and flatware, and all through the night more arrived. Apparently at any given moment, one or more groups of people were having a meal – or a banquet – in this castle.

Athena tried to picture these lavish events. Was it like the Renaissance paintings she'd seen of European royalty? Long, long tables piled high with every sort of food in the world, spoiled aristocrats greedily reaching for it with their grubby fingers? Or were they more refined events, with sophisticated dukes and earls daintily holding out their pinkies while they delicately nibbled on a pelican drumstick…

Amy elbowed Athena, knocking her out of her reverie. "Time to go!"

After what had seemed to Athena to be just a few hours of work, their 12-hour stint was indeed over. The day shift was marching in, ready to take over. Athena's team stepped away from the dishwashing table and started back to the dorms. Athena hustled to catch up to Tyro. She tapped her on the arm: "Please, tell me about Irina."

Tyro looked around to see if Irina was within earshot, but Irina was moving more slowly, several paces behind. Tyro leaned in close and whispered, "I don't know very much. Like most of us, she doesn't really have any family. But I heard that she was caught trying to escape, and when they brought her back they… did things to her. Things that changed her, made her like this."
Athena was appalled. "What kind of things?"

Tyro shrugged. "Triton's got a lot of power, especially in that trident of his. Even if he didn't physically punish her, he could have gotten inside her head and messed her up.

She never talks about it; she might not even remember it herself. But I've seen her in the morning, just sitting and staring up at the sun, when she really ought to be sleeping." Tyro shook her head. "But that's the case with all of us. 'Foundlings.' We're all a little messed up one way or another, right? I mean, look at you, with that crazy get-up."

Athena forced a smile, acknowledging that she was dressed like a crazy person, at least in this world. She walked/ swam with Tyro for a bit longer, then slowed her pace and allowed Tyro to drift away. Athena settled into a stride that got her closer to Irina.

She had a million things she wanted to say, to ask, but she didn't want to scare off this obviously troubled woman. Plus really, how could this be her mother? She died eight long years ago. Athena decided to act casual.

"Hey, Irina."
"Hey…"
"Good shift?"
Irina shrugged. "Same as usual, I suppose."
"So, how long have you been here?"
"All my life."
"Really? You never… left? Did any traveling?"
Irina seemed to wince at the question, or possibly at a memory. "I don't… think so."

Athena forced a smile. "Oh, you'd remember if you'd traveled! There's a whole big world out there, right?"
"Not for us," and with that, Irina shut down. *No further questions*, her furrowed brow told Athena.

They continued on in silence for a while. As they got closer to the dorms, Irina quietly said, "I used to dream of visiting the surface."

"Dream?"

Irina nodded. "In my dreams, I'd swim straight up toward the light, break the surface of the water, and breathe the fresh air. I'd walk on dry land, and everything would feel different on my skin, from the warmth of the sun, to the cool of a breeze."

"That sounds really nice…"

Irina nodded, slightly smiling at the reverie. "I'd meet a man, someone kind and loving. He would hold me in his arms and it would feel entirely different from anything I'd ever known down here."

"Would you stay up there forever?"

Irina shook her head. "No, I'd come and go, freely. I love the sea; I'd never want to leave. But the freedom, to go back and forth…"

"Irina, are you sure… you never did it? That it was all just dreams?"

Irina stopped and turned to Athena. She stared deeply into her eyes, for the first time, really. "What do you mean?"

Athena looked left and right; they were just a few doors down from her tiny dormitory. "Will you come into my room for a minute?"

Irina was clearly suspicious, but she agreed to go with the girl. They moved toward the entrance, and Athena checked again to make sure no one was watching before she closed the door behind them. They sat down on the bed.

"I'm Athena. Does the name mean *anything* to you?"

"I've known many Athena's. It's a popular name, although she did defeat Lord Poseidon."

"How about Robert Crowley?"

Irina blinked a few times, and sat up straighter.

"I… there's something. I don't know. Who is he?"

"My father."

Something deep inside Irina's mind was working its way toward the surface, but there was much debris blocking it. Too much?

"Irina… I don't know what happened to you, to your memory… but what if I told you that you really *did* make it to the surface? That you *did* meet a man… you did have a child?"

Irina's head shook back and forth. Her lips moved, but she didn't say anything. Her hands came up to her face, but her fingers were trembling. "I don't – who are you – why are you – I don't know…"

Athena gently put a hand on Irina's knee. "It doesn't make any sense to me, either. But you look exactly like my mother. My mother Irina. When I was three she… disappeared into the sea. But I have pictures, and I know from – "

And suddenly Athena remembered – her locket!

Her hands shaking, Athena managed to get the chain from around her neck. She opened the locket, and showed the tiny photos inside to Irina: Baby Athena on the left, beautiful young Irina on the right.

As Irina stared silently at the pictures, Athena observed a physical change in her. The brow became less furrowed, the frown less permanent, and the clouds seemed to lift from her eyes. The little photographs unlocked a flood of memories, and in the rush of recollection Irina's true personality returned to her. Within moments, this tormented woman once again became Athena's living, breathing, mother.

# Chapter 23

Robert Crowley paced nervously in the Miami airport, waiting for his flight to Nassau.

He had gotten up early – he'd barely slept anyway – and once again called everybody he knew on Paradise Island. No one had yet seen nor heard from Athena. And last night, when Mrs. Lucy had gone to their house, Athena hadn't been there. Not sleeping with headphones on, not in Robert's room, not anywhere. In fact, there was no sign that she'd come home at all.

So the moment he got off the phone with Mrs. Lucy, he went online and booked a trip home on the first possible flight which, unfortunately, was not until 6:30 a.m. He made a few apologies to some associates at the conference, and caught the first flight from Mexico City to Miami. Now there was the "puddle jumper" to Nassau, and a friend at Atlantis had arranged for a helicopter to take him immediately to the resort when his plane landed.

Robert had used every spare moment in his travels to arrange for search parties on land and at sea. Some were already starting, but for him the search would begin in earnest once he arrived.

He just hoped it wasn't too late. It *couldn't* be too late. He couldn't go through this… again.

\*     \*     \*

Irina was hugging Athena so tightly she thought she might crack a rib… and she didn't care. Her mother! Mom! *Mommy!*

Are there words to describe the joy, the relief, the bitter-sweet pain Athena felt at this moment? She had long ago learned to live without a mother, but she'd never stopped yearning for her. It had been pointless to hope. Her mother was drowned. Dead and gone. And so she had accepted that and moved on.

But now, here she was. Here *they* were, in this tiny room, deep, deep in the ocean, hugging each other so hard an observer might think they were wrestling. Crying and laughing in the same heaving breaths.

And when they finally separated, to once again look at each other, drinking in the bliss of each other's faces, they barely knew where to begin.

Athena stuttered, "How? What happened?"

"I'm not quite sure. Triton – he did something. He pointed that trident at me and… I wasn't myself any longer. I just vanished… in here." She tapped the side of her head. "I don't know how he did it."

"But why? How did… I mean – " Athena simply didn't know where to begin.

Irina gently took hold of her hands. "Triton is my grandfather. Even though I'm a biped, I share royal blood. I was in a rare, exalted position among the humans. But I dreamed… I wanted to visit the surface. And it was forbidden. So I went anyway."

Irina shook her head. "I haven't thought about any of this in so long. I haven't remembered! But this –" She held up the locket. "And you! It's all coming back to me."

Athena could barely contain herself. "What happened next?"

"I learned to wait until Grandfather was away, and I would slip out of Atlantica unnoticed. The guards didn't circle overhead in those days. Or I would say I was going treasure hunting… I knew of a sunken ship near Eleuthera where I could always take a few things shortly before returning home, to support my story.

"I spent enough time among the land dwellers that I began to form relationships. They accepted me as one of their own, and I loved them. Eventually… I met your father. I first saw him working deep under the water and I found him fascinating. I followed his team back to the surface, and figured out some silly way to meet him. I think I even asked for directions!

"I had never known anyone so brilliant and yet so kind. He was funny – or goofy, I don't know – but he made me laugh. And I fell in love with him."

Athena smiled at images of her mother and father falling innocently in love. It warmed her from the inside, starting in her heart and spreading throughout her body. Her mother gave her hands a squeeze and continued.

"I was still going back and forth between Nassau and Atlantica, but it was getting more difficult… harder to get away from Atlantica, and harder still to be away from Robert. So I decided to leave, once and for all. I began to spread stories about a giant creature I'd caught a glimpse of, the likes of which no one had ever seen before. They couldn't have – because I made it up.

"It was sort of cross between a whale and a crocodile. Huge, with a powerful tail and enormous, razor sharp teeth. I announced that I simply had to have a better look at it and so, against everyone's better judgment, I went to seek it out.

"When I didn't return for days, they sent out search parties. After a week or two they found what I had been wearing – what I'd left for them to find – some jewels, my wrap – and determined that I had been killed by this creature. It served a double purpose; not only was my disappearance accepted, but it also became one more reason to never leave the safety of Atlantica – there were sea monsters lurking in the water!"

She laughed at the memory… and then darkened at thoughts of what came later.

"I returned to Nassau, to my Robert. We were married, and life was bliss. Our time together was magical, everything I'd ever dreamed about. Years passed in the blink of an eye."

She hugged Athena once again. "And then you came and my happiness was complete."

Athena grew warm and happy picturing her earliest days. Irina continued, "But as you remember, we would frequently go to the sea. And it happened that one day several of my half-sisters – mermaids – were following a small ship. Playing, really, that's all they were doing. I think they'd spotted a boy they found handsome. Naturally this was also against the rules, for if land dwellers were to learn that mermaids truly exist, there'd be no peace under the sea for all time."

Athena remembered that once, some tourists had spotted a few mermaids near Atlantis and had photographed them… but Athena always thought it was a publicity stunt of some kind.

She was stunned to learn they were actually wayward mermaids breaking the rules of the undersea world!

"Anyway, they were busy gossiping about the boy, when you fell into the water. Do you remember? One of them saw us, and reported back to Triton. He sent a terrible whirlpool to literally pull me away from your father, and…" She began to cry softly. "That poor man. He must have thought I was dead. I'd never told him the truth about my family… I didn't know how to at first, and later, I just wanted to forget it myself. And you… I never thought that you might…" She looked up at Athena.

Athena suddenly became aware of a stinging sensation in her eyes. She was crying, too, and hadn't even realized it. One of the effects of being underwater… you don't feel your tears flowing.

Irina continued, "I'm so sorry to have left you. A girl needs her mother, and I wasn't there for you. I was so selfish to have even come to the surface in the first place, thinking only of my own happiness. I'm so sorry…"

They held each other for a while, crying softly and stroking each other's hair. Eventually they calmed themselves, and Irina continued her story.

"I was brought before Triton on my knees. He was furious with me; I'd never seen him so angry. Never! I knew he'd enslave me, but I never dreamed he'd go so far as to… but you see, he wanted to make an example of me. To show everyone – you don't leave Atlantica! And he knew I'd try to escape, if I could, to return to you and Robert. So he aimed his trident at me and… I don't even know what he did. But now, sitting here with you, I don't have any memories of the time between that day and this moment."

# Chapter 24

From the helicopter, Robert could see a number of boats in the waters off Paradise Island. He knew some were just tourists and yachting enthusiasts, but he also knew that at least six were searching for Athena. Two were police boats. One was a research vessel with a remote-controlled submersible sending video images back to its captain. Dexter was piloting another boat, with a team of volunteer divers ready to leap into the water on a moment's notice. And the others were friends in smaller motorboats, scanning the water with binoculars and calling out Athena's name over and over.

Robert's plan was to jump into his boat the moment the helicopter landed, to get out there and join the search. But something flashed through his mind just as the helicopter touched down. Shouldn't he apply the Scientific Method to this search, as he applied it to every search he'd undertaken in his career?

There had to be clues, some indication somewhere of where Athena had gone, or what she was doing. Perhaps there was a record of her signing out a piece of equipment… maybe she'd emailed a friend about her plans… maybe she'd left a note for him that Mrs. Lucy hadn't seen!

In that instant, he decided to change course: he'd go home and scour the place for evidence, some trace to guide him to his daughter.

*         *         *

Athena gripped Irina's hands, knowing their only hope was to escape from Triton's watery kingdom. "We have to get out of here! We have to get you home, to daddy."

"Oh, darling, I don't think so."

"And these slaves! It's the twenty-first century. There's no more slavery. Or there shouldn't be, anyway."

"Athena darling, this is a different world. This way of life has existed unchanged for thousands of years."

"So? The world changes. The Pharaohs ruled Egypt for thousands of years, and now they have a democracy there."

"This isn't Egypt, my sweet. It's an underwater city ruled by a demi-god with divine powers. But... I agree. It's no place for you. I have to figure out a way for you to escape."

"For both of us to escape!"

"Yes, of course. Both of us." Irina looked away for a moment. She didn't want Athena to see a flicker of doubt in her eyes.

Irina spoke firmly, "For now, get some rest. You haven't slept in a long time, and you'll need your energy. I'll come get you before the start of tonight's shift and we'll see what we can do."

Athena felt ready to cry again. "Can't you stay here with me? The bed's big enough..."

Irina had spent such a long time alone in the darkness of forgetfulness that it hadn't even occurred to her to sleep with Athena.

The two of them curled up together as close as two teaspoons in a drawer, reveling in the love and warmth emanating from the other. They were asleep in minutes.

*         *         *

Archibald was beyond exhausted, but he wasn't going to stop now.

From the moment Athena was taken away by the large merman, he did his best to track her movements. He swam back and forth, peering into the barred windows of Triton's castle. He inquired after her with any fish he met who swam through the castle halls.

He now understood that she had been made a member of the castle's staff of enslaved bipeds, and so he swam relentlessly, back and forth, trying to catch a glimpse of her or, better yet, find her alone somewhere. He even dared to enter the castle once when he thought he spotted her… but it was another slave girl. He had to locate her. He finally had a plan, but time was running out.

*     *     *

Robert stood in the doorway of Athena's bedroom, scanning. He looked for anything new he didn't recognize, and anything important that might be missing. His first search revealed nothing, so he began again. He went to her equipment chest. Inside were her cleats, some balls, bats, racquets… but wait – her snorkeling gear was missing!

Alright then, he reasoned. She went snorkeling somewhere. But with whom? Dexter had not heard from her. Did she go with a friend? She certainly wouldn't have gone alone.

His gaze drifted to her desk. Her cellphone! She'd left without it. That was strange. Maybe there was a message, or a clue in the list of sent or received calls. He flipped through the menus, but the only messages were from him and Sheridan, all inquiring about where she was. Other than that, there was nothing to indicate where she'd gone, or with whom.

However… there, on the left hand side, was her journal. He knew that she didn't write in it often, but he gave a little prayer that she'd written something before leaving yesterday morning. He grabbed it and started flipping through the pages. He felt terrible invading her privacy like this, but it was a true emergency.

He reached the final page, where Athena had written about meeting Archibald on Thursday. She hadn't put down much. She'd written about speaking with the fish and other sea creatures, about her glee at finally understanding the reason for the loud noise which always plagued her under water, and about her anticipation of spending more time with Archibald "tomorrow."

Clutching the book, Robert sat down on the bed. What was the meaning of this? Was Athena working on a story? It had to be, but all her previous tales were about characters she'd made up; they were never about herself. She'd written this as a diary entry, like the rest of the journal. It was obviously pure fantasy… perhaps related to the long ago memory of that awful day when she claimed a barracuda had spoken to her as her life nearly slipped away.

Still, it was a clue. She'd clearly stated that she was meeting Archibald again, Friday afternoon at the Grotto. So Robert Crowley would start his search there.

# Chapter 25

Athena was deeply asleep, dreaming a sweet dream… a memory from childhood…

She and both her parents were at the Fish Fry over on New Providence. Hundreds of people were gathered there to practice for Junkanoo – the massive Christmas parade down Bay Street in Nassau – and the scene was overwhelming. Scores of drummers, dozens of horn players, singers, dancers, revelers of all kinds were making music and a joyful noise. Except in the dream, Athena wasn't a little girl, she was her current age, and her parents were back together, after so many years apart. Athena was smiling in her sleep…

"Athena, wake up! Wake up!"

A hoarse whisper slowly worked its way through Athena's unconscious brain and into her dream. Now, in Nassau, she was looking around, wondering who was calling her. She could barely hear the voice above the cacophony of the Junkanoo rehearsal. "Hello?" she called out. "Where are you?"

"Athena, I'm at the window. Please wake up!"

Confused, Athena finally stirred from her slumber and began to remember… she wasn't in Nassau… she was in bed, in Triton's castle, a prisoner… but with her mother!

She turned around – yes, Irina was still there beside her, asleep. "...*at the window*..." Athena looked up. Archibald was there, at the window, his little face peering between the bars!

"Athena, thank goodness. I've been looking for you since yesterday. Who's that with you?"
"My mother!"
"But I thought you said she – "
"I was wrong." Athena hopped out of the bed and rushed to the window. "She – she's from here. She's Triton's grand-daughter."
"Ah." Archibald spent a moment processing this new information. It certainly answered a lot of questions! But there was no time for further consideration.

"I've been working on getting you out of here," he told Athena, "and I have a plan. But we have to hurry. Triton's been away. He returned a short while ago and went directly to bed."

Athena took this in, as Archibald continued breathily, "There's a little-used gate about one hundred-fifty lengths from the rear entrance of the administration wing. I noticed last night that just after the shift change, it was briefly unguarded. If we get there at exactly right moment, you might slip away unnoticed."
"What time is it now?"
"I think the chime will sound fairly soon. You should get ready."
Athena nodded, and turned back toward the bed.

She gently placed a hand on her mother's shoulder, and softly pushed back and forth, whispering, "Mother? Mom... time to wake up."

Irina slowly stirred. Like Athena, she was at first a bit confused by her surroundings. She gathered herself in a moment and threw her arms around Athena.

"Darling, how did you sleep?"

"Great. Mom, this is Archibald, my friend." She guided Irina to the window, where the woman and the turtle greeted each other without touching, as most sea creatures do.

Athena told Irina Archibald's plan, pausing only to ask how long a "length" was (the length of Triton's arm, as it happens – roughly three feet) and then said, "Now what about the rest of the people?"

Archibald squinted at her. "What do you mean?"

"These people, like my mother, and Tyro, and Aithra, and all the children. They're slaves. We can't leave them here."

Archibald was silent. It was Irina who spoke. "Athena, this is not your fight."

"Of course it is. These are my people. *Your* people."

"But this has been a way of life for –"

"For too long! It's time to put an end to this. Mom, c'mon. *Slavery?* In the 21st Century?"

"This is a different world, my darling. Not your world."

"No, that's not true. I'm *your* daughter. I can live and breathe under water. I can talk to fish and turtles and all the rest of them. This *is* my world. This *is* my fight."

Irina sighed, defeated, yet also proud of her brave daughter. "Fine. Then it *is* your fight. But it's a battle for another day. When we've made plans, and gathered resources. Right now, we have to get you out of here and back home to your father. He needs you more than ever, Athena."

"*And* you."

"Yes, and me."

Athena stuck out her hand, and her mother took it.

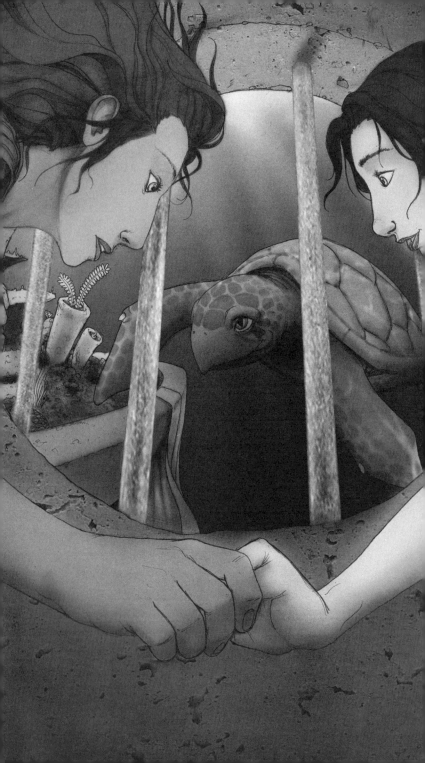

They shook, sealing the agreement. Athena turned back to Archibald. "Okay. What do we do now?"

"There's a storage area near the gate. If you can get there unnoticed, you can hide until just before the shift change, and then wait for my signal."
"What's the signal?"
Archibald almost smiled once more, "You'll know."

*     *     *

Robert had taken his boat to the grotto. Against his better judgment, he'd convinced himself he might find Athena sitting there, chatting with a turtle. But if she had been taken out to sea by a current, he wanted to be ready to follow after her.

He threw his dock line up onto the big rock, and clambered out of the boat. He splashed into the grotto – but there was nothing there. Just a few fish lingering in the bottom, who seemed quite disturbed by his presence. There was no sign of Athena.

He climbed up the big rock and scanned the area. There – back on the path, was Athena's bicycle. So she *had* been here! This was the place to begin the search. Robert pulled out his cell phone and called Dexter and the several other friends who were still actively looking for Athena. He told them to hurry over to the tip of the island in their boats… and to make sure their flashlights were charged. The sun was sinking into the horizon. It would soon be night.

Robert ground his teeth. Looking for a young girl in the big ocean was hard enough; doing it at night was virtually impossible.

# Chapter 26

Archibald told them how to find the little storage area, and then swam away to finish making arrangements. Athena and Irina hugged once more, and nodded at each other decisively. Athena said, "This is it… no turning back now!"

She carefully opened her dorm room door – the hallway was empty. So far, so good. They followed Archibald's directions… down the dormitory hallway, turn right and pass through another section of workers' rooms, down a level to a service corridor, and then across the administrative wing. That would be the most dangerous stretch, for they had no legitimate reason to be there.

Just as they entered the service corridor, two big guards exited the mermen's bathroom, heading in Athena and Irina's direction. Athena felt the hairs on the back of her neck stand up. Irina's hand tightened around hers. *Just keep going*, she thought to herself. *Don't give anything away…*

They cast their gazes downward, not wanting to even make eye contact with the guards. They drew closer and closer to each other… and passed! The guards either hadn't noticed them, or didn't care or –

"You two!"

*Oh, no!*

"Just keep going," Irina whispered forcefully to her daughter. But the smaller of the two guards called out again, more loudly, "You two! Stop right there."

They had to stop. The guards were upon them in an instant. The smaller one spoke first: "Where are you going?"
"She's ill," Irina answered. "I'm taking her to see the nurse."
"She looks old enough to go by herself."
"She's my daughter, sir. I want to make sure she's all right."
"You want to make sure to cut your shift short, more like it." Both guards laughed. The bigger one reached a hand down and grabbed Athena's chin. He tilted her face up to examine her.

She was so tired and fearful it was easy to believe she was ill. He dropped her chin and said, "Fine, be on your way. But you're on duty until the chime sounds, so get back to work once you've delivered her to the nurse."
"Yes, sir. Of course. Thank you sir," Irina responded with all the humility she could muster. The guards turned and continued on their way, so Irina and Athena did the same.

The rest of their journey went without incident, and in a short while they were hiding behind several crates, under a tarp, waiting for Archibald's signal. About 30 yards along the path was the gate, attended by two low-level guards. Although they were too far away for Athena to hear what they were saying, the guards were clearly bored and marking time.

Every few minutes someone passed the hiding place; a slave on an errand, or a guard moving toward his shift. Athena overheard a few comments – people were chattering excitedly about Triton's homecoming.

He had been away for some weeks and his arrival always signaled the start of a celebration in which most citizens participated. Athena whispered to Irina, "I'd like to see Triton. I'd tell him a thing or two about how he runs his city…" but her mother shushed her and they continued to wait in silence.

They huddled tight in the small space, holding each other. It was warm, but they shivered anyway. As they waited, it grew darker and darker. Up, high above in the open air world, the sun was setting.

\*       \*       \*

"Athena!"
"*Athena!*"
Robert stood in the center of his little boat, calling out his daughter's name. He continuously scanned the surface of the water with his high-beam light.

Dexter piloted a boat nearby, and there were two more boats in the area. The search party shone their lights across the water and shouted for the missing girl. They'd been at it over an hour.

Dexter called out, "Robert, are you planning to stay out all night?"
Robert nodded.
Dexter sighed, tired and more than a little frustrated.
"Mightn't it make more sense to get some rest, and come back at first light?"
"I don't know, Dexter. It might. But I can't leave. I… by all means, if you need a break, please, go take one. I understand, I do."
"If you're staying, I'm staying."

Robert smiled weakly, his heart filled with gratitude.

While Dexter felt overcome with despair, he wasn't going to let Robert know that. He knew from experience that Athena rarely wore a life vest – you really had to force her – and if she'd been washed out to sea without one, there was almost no chance she could have survived this many hours in the water.

*     *     *

Athena noticed a growing clamor, as though a large group of tourists was about to pass. She snuck her head up and saw a vast school of yellow jacks approaching. There were thousands of them!

The guards at the gate waved their spears at the fish, and the yellow jacks backed away. Athena could hear the guards laughing. The giant school approached the gate again, and this time the guards half-heartedly attempted to spear some fish – but the yellow jacks were too fast and avoided getting stuck. The school pulled back into the darkness. Athena watched this bizarre scene, transfixed.

One of the guards yawned, stretched his muscled arms, and looked up toward the surface. Athena guessed he made some sort of comment about the time. And then, as if on cue, the gong sounded.

The guards looked left and right, and even though they did not see their replacements coming, they turned and swam away from the gate. Once they were gone, the enormous school of yellow jacks was back; some of the fish nearly nosing through the gate.

Still watching them, Athena heard them whisper as one: "Now!"

This was the signal. She grabbed Irina's hand and they made their way toward the gate as fast as they could.

# Chapter 27

Robert Crowley was so very tired; he had been up for two days, and the exhaustion and stress were taking their toll.

So when he saw a figure break the surface of the water about a hundred feet away, he could scarcely believe his eyes.

"Athena?"

He fired up his boat's engine and headed in the direction of the splash. Dexter saw what he was up to and decided to follow.

Keeping the light steady while piloting the boat was difficult. He saw the figure rise again and splash back into the water. Robert's heart rose up to his throat, as he hoped against hope it was Athena, still alive, still swimming.

He got to within a few yards of the spot, and waited… and waited… and then – he saw a figure splashing at the surface of the water –

A dolphin. It was just a dolphin, playing. Robert sat down on the little seat in his boat, utterly defeated. He put his face in his hands, and began to cry. He wept as he hadn't wept since Irina was taken from him. He felt himself giving up hope, felt that this was more painful than he could bear.

As if in response to his sobs, the dolphin called out, "Ack – ka – ka – ka – kah! Ack – ka – ka – ka – kah!"
Robert looked up.

The dolphin was half out of the water, using its powerful tail fin to stay upright. The creature looked straight at him, calling out. Robert stopped crying and looked back at the animal. Was it… *talking* to him? Quietly, he repeated, "Athena?"

The dolphin whistled, and then once again cackled, "Ack – ka – ka – ka – kah! Ka – ka – kaaaaah!" And with that, it splashed back into the water, and shot right back up again. Then it leapt about five feet through the air and splashed into the water, circling back and holding itself upright again. As Robert watched, the dolphin repeated this action, each time moving a little further away from his boat before circling back.

Dumbfounded, he said aloud, "It wants me to follow it."

As if in response, the dolphin was suddenly joined by a second, and the two of them repeated the leaping and circling action in unison.

Robert called out, "Alright, I'll follow you. Show me the way!" He gunned the motor and steered after the dolphins, who were leaping and swimming further out to sea.

*     *     *

Archibald was waiting right outside the gate, hidden behind the low wall. He fairly shouted, "Hurry! Athena, get on my back."

Athena got hold of Archibald's shell and held on tight. He pushed his way to the center of the school, Irina following closely behind. Athena could see immediately that her mother was a strong swimmer. *Of course she is!* she thought. The yellow jacks closed ranks tightly around the trio, and the entire group began to swim away from the castle.

Just at that moment, the night-shift guards arrived at the gate. They were actually brothers, Picumnus and Pilumnus, who'd spent their whole lives doing everything together – school, sports, and now work. They peered at the enormous school swimming away, turned to each other and said, "That's odd."

Pilumnus continued, "They look like they're running away, don't they?"

His brother responded, "You think they stole something?"

"Well, I've never really trusted yellow jacks, have you?"

"Never."

"You check if anybody's missing anything, and I'll follow them."

"Good plan."

So Pilumnus took off after the yellow jacks, and Picumnus headed into the castle. The hallways were abuzz with activity as the shift change was in full swing. Picumnus swam around all the young bipeds rushing to their work stations and headed for the Supply Chief, to ask if any food or other items had gone missing.

*       *       *

Melora, meanwhile, was overseeing the shift change. She kept an eagle eye out for Athena, confident that the newest foundling would oversleep. She'd have to make an example of her... too bad, she seemed like a decent girl. Still, Melora loved making examples of people. She swam up to the girl's room and even smiled to herself when she saw the door still closed. *Right again,* she thought. *As always.* She pulled the door open with a flourish, calling out "Wakey, wakey!" but was surprised to see no one in the bed.

Within moments she confirmed that Athena was indeed missing – no one had seen her. But stranger still, Irina was missing as well. Melora's mind worked quickly… she did a little figuring…

"No," she said to herself. "It can't be…"
As one of the few who knew Irina's true identity, Melora knew she had to do something no one in Atlantica ever wanted to do: she had to wake Triton with bad news.

*    *    *

The dolphins were leading Robert further and further out to sea. He had his motor going full-throttle just to keep up with them. Dexter, who was following as well, had fallen quite a ways behind.

Robert's cell phone buzzed. He didn't want to bother answering, but it was Dexter calling. Struggling to keep a hand on vibrating the steering wheel, Robert managed to open the phone.
"Yes?"
"Where are you going?"
"I don't know."
"Can you slow down? I can't keep up."
"No… I don't want to lose them."
"Who?
"The dolphins."
"*Who?* It sounded like you said –"
"Dolphins. They're taking me somewhere. I think they're taking me to Athena."

Dexter looked at the phone in his hand. So, Robert had snapped. The grief and sleeplessness had cracked him open, and now he was chasing dolphins. Well, Dexter realized, *I don't have a choice.* He had to follow, and be ready to rescue Robert when he gave up or ran out of gas – whichever came first.

*     *     *

Athena was positively giddy. She was in the middle of a thrilling escape, riding on the shell of her brilliant and powerful friend, her mother swimming at her side, surrounded by thousands of glistening allies. What an adventure!

It never occurred to her to look behind them. But Irina did; she stole a glance and caught the tiniest glimpse of Pilumnus. He was keeping a discreet distance, holding steady just the same, firmly on their tail. She turned back, forced herself to smile at Athena, and pressed on. This was all going to end one of only two ways, she realized, and there was nothing she could do about that now.

# Chapter 28

"**W**hat?"

There was no other sound under the sea quite like the big, booming roar which emerged from King Triton when angered. And he was very angry now.

He towered over Melora as he rose from his bed. He was a mammoth merman, with a chest like a refrigerator and arms like maple trees. He had a thick white beard and a long, wild mane of silvery-white hair. It was impossible to tell how old he was; the deep-set lines in his face and the gray of his hair indicated he had many years on this earth. But he possessed the vitality and strength of a much younger man. He was, in a word, terrifying.

He barked at her, "How could you have let this happen?" Melora was trembling. "I didn't realize who she was, your highness. I'm so sorry."

"*Sorry!*" The word echoed around his huge bed chamber. He didn't need to say any more.

He reigned in his temper momentarily. "Where are they now?"

"Pilumnus, the guard, is following them."
"Good. At least he was thinking." Leaning against the wall near Triton's bed was his trident. It was ancient, yet still shimmered an unearthly gold. It contained the power of a god, and Triton could wield it mercilessly.

The King of Atlantica grabbed his trident and swam quickly out of the room. Melora watched him go, temporarily relieved. Yet she knew that if Irina and the girl were not recovered, she would be in for an ocean of trouble.

Within moments, Triton was at the rear gate of his castle, where Picumnus was waiting. Triton moved quickly; the guards following had a difficult time keeping up.

*"Where?"*
Picumnus recoiled a bit from Triton's intimidating growl. Indeed, he didn't speak at all in response, but merely pointed the direction in which the school of yellow jacks had gone.

Triton turned to his guards. "Fan out in all directions. The fish could be a diversion, and they may have gone elsewhere. I want them found, and I want them *unharmed*. Their punishment is my concern."

With a powerful flap of his huge tail, Triton took off, several of his faster guards following as they could, not keeping up.

*     *     *

Athena knew that Archibald was swimming with all his might. He was fast, but he was old, and this effort was taking a toll on him. She leaned over and spoke into his ear, "Why don't you take a break?"
Huffing and puffing, he responded, "I don't think that's a very good idea. They could be following us already."
Athena craned her neck around to look behind them. She didn't see anything but a thousand yellow jacks.
"Where are we going?"
"To meet your father, I hope."

*     *     *

Robert was still following the dolphins at top speed. It worried him that he was heading farther out to sea, but he felt in his gut that this was the right thing to do. He did wonder, *Where are they taking me?* but he could not stop. He would not stop. He had a spare fuel tank, so he could go as far as –

The dolphins came to a standstill. They reared up in the water, treading on their tails and chattered loudly. They seemed to be telling him, *this is the spot.* But he didn't see anything. He shut off his motor and frantically began scanning the area with his light. *Please, please…* he uttered a quiet prayer, hoping against all hope that this chase had not been in vain.

\*        \*        \*

Triton caught up to Pilumnus, who indicated the school of yellow jacks up ahead. Triton nodded at him, which was as close to a compliment as the guard could expect. He reverently fell back as Triton swam closer to the massive school of fish.

"*Halt,*" he called out in his booming voice.

The fish continued to race away from him, and up toward the surface of the water. They had defied him!

"I said, **halt!**" The word carried through the water like a torpedo.

Athena had been holding tightly to Archibald, her head pressed down onto his shell to cut down on drag. She heard a bellow, and thought *what was that?* It almost sounded like words, but no one had a voice like that.

Before she could ask Archibald about it, he called out to her, "Hold on! We've got to get out of here."

The turtle, tired as he was, put everything he had into picking up speed. He believed that if he could get to the surface, the girl might be safe…

When Triton saw that he was being disobeyed, he flicked his trident, and a powerful ripple spread out into the waters around him. First it hit his guards, who were all knocked out of their strides, even while struggling to catch up to him. Then it reached the yellow jacks.

Athena was nearly shaken off Archibald's shell. It took all her strength to hold on. "What was that? What's going on?" she yelled, but Archibald did not answer.

Irina called out to him, "We need to stop, Archibald."
"No, if we can make it to the surface then –"
"He can kill us all, Archibald. Surely you know that."

Archibald didn't respond except to squint his eyes and swim even faster. Athena craned her neck around to see what was going on behind them. She caught her first glimpse of the terrible king of the sea. He was beyond anything she had imagined him to be.

Triton watched the group attempt to escape him. *What could they be thinking?* he wondered. *I'll send these fools to the crushing black depths.*

He raised his trident and carefully took aim. Concentrating as he was, he didn't see a dark shape emerging from the blackness of the deep sea. He didn't feel the subtle shift in current as the creature approached. And he wasn't the slightest bit ready when the winged giant slammed into him, knocking the trident from his hand and sending him reeling.

Athena shouted, "Zeus!"

It was Zeus. The ray had stayed close by the resort, keeping an eye on Athena. Seeing his moment to help her escape, he acted boldly – attacking Triton himself! Surely Zeus was one of the bravest creatures ever to swim the sea.

Athena watched as Triton raced downwards, towards the sinking trident. "You'll pay for that, beast!" he called out as Zeus vanished into the darkness as quickly as he had appeared.

Archibald called out, "Hold on, Athena. We've go to go!" "Okay!" Athena stuck her head down, and Archibald continued on. The yellow jacks closed in tighter than ever, and the group raced to the surface.

But Irina stopped swimming. She dropped out of the group and waited in the spot, turning to watch as Triton retrieved his trident and positioned himself to attack once more. He looked up and saw his granddaughter alone, her companions racing away without her. He raised his trident to fire at the group –

"No!" Irina screamed, and now she swam with all her might to face the mighty Triton.
"Grandfather, please don't hurt them."
"You dare to defy me?"
"No, sir. I beg you for mercy."

Triton frowned, gazing with some confusion at the young woman. Once, long ago, Irina had been his favorite grandchild. She'd had a spirit, a lightness, which amused him no end. He had bounced her on his knee, stroking her black hair, kissing her tiny feet, watching her spin in a miniature whirlpool of his creation… he'd told her stories of the ancient gods and heroes… taught her skills that few mortals knew…

And then one day she'd betrayed him, breaking the most sacred law of Atlantica. He'd had no choice but to punish her as he would have punished anyone who attempted to leave the city and endanger their entire world.

"Grandfather, my daughter is a land dweller. It's the only life she's ever known. She came here yesterday by accident, guided by a friendly turtle who meant no harm. Please let her go."
"She'll speak of Atlantica. She'll guide the air breathers here, and then we'll have war."
"No sir, she won't do that. She just wants to go home to her father, my beloved."

Triton winced at the memory. To him it was only yesterday that his own flesh and blood, his Irina, had snuck away to marry a land dweller!

"Grandfather I've paid for my transgression, haven't I? And hasn't Robert, in losing his wife? He's innocent, sir. He knows nothing of our world – I never told him a thing, you know that."

Irina put her hand on Triton's arm. "Is it right for him to lose his daughter as he lost his wife? When he's done nothing but work his entire career to protect the sea, to serve the creatures who live in it, and to honor the history of our people with his research?"

Triton glared at her, unforgiving.
"Sir, I beg you."

# Chapter 29

Archibald and Athena reached the surface, crashing through the waves into the moonlit night, only yards away from where Robert still sat in his boat, pondering his lonely future.

Athena coughed out the water in her lungs and gasped for air as Archibald helped her stay afloat. She had difficulty adjusting her eyes back to the air-filled world.

Robert could not believe what he was seeing. He remained frozen for seconds, watching what he reasoned must be a hallucination.

Athena managed to croak out, "Daddy!"

Robert snapped awake. He flew into the water and was by Athena's side in a heartbeat. He took her into his arms, keeping her head above water, and pulled her through the waves back to his boat. Archibald floated nearby, watching. The yellow jacks had scattered.

Finding strength he'd never known, Robert hauled himself and Athena into the boat with one arm. She was breathing normally – not drowning. He didn't understand how, but he was grateful. He wrapped a dry blanket around her and held her tight, held her with all his being.

"Athena…Athena," he repeated. "My darling, I thought I'd lost you…"

"Daddy… daddy… where's mommy?"

Robert's heart skipped a beat – had she suffered some kind memory loss? He thought, *If she's gone too long without oxygen, it could have injured her brain.* He realized had to get her back to a hospital before –

Athena was instantly clear-eyed and wide awake. She grabbed his arm: "She was right here. Right next to me. Do you see her?" Athena stood up and began looking around.
"Athena, your mother – "
"Daddy, she's alive. I was *just with* her."

Athena leaned over the side of the boat, calling out, "Mom! Mommy!" She spotted the flashlight and grabbed it, beaming it onto the water this way and that, trying urgently to catch sight of her. "*Mom!*" she shrieked, desperately.

"Athena."

It was Irina's voice. Athena whipped around, aiming the light. And there, in the water, was her mother, swimming toward the boat.

Robert's head was reeling. Nothing he was witnessing was possible, and yet… here it was. Had he died? Was he asleep, dreaming?

"Irina!" He leaned to pull her into the boat. Athena ran to his side.
"No, darling, I can't," Irina said gently. "Just listen to me."
"I – please, Irina…" He stretched out his hand. When she would not take it, he jumped into the water and swam to her.

Athena watched as they embraced. And even as they kissed, she couldn't turn away. She understood what her father wanted; a way to somehow make up for eight long, lost years.

To show Irina that he loved her as much as he ever did. Athena knew better than anyone that Robert Crowley had never stopped missing his wife.

After a long moment, Irina gently pulled away from her husband and said, "Robert, take Athena home. Now."
"Of course. Let's go."
"No. I -- I can't come with you."
"Irina –"
"Robert, I can't."
"I don't understand."

Irina sighed, and with a calmness Robert would always remember, said, "Many years ago, I broke a sacred vow to be with you. And I paid the ultimate price. I lost my husband, my daughter, my life. And now… The only way you and Athena will survive is if I go back willingly now."

Athena realized what Irina had done. The bargain she had struck. But her father couldn't understand.
"No. No, I won't let you," Robert said forcefully. "We're getting in this boat together and –"
"Robert, the man to whom I am beholden is a king of the ocean. We'd never outrun him. He has almost limitless powers. He can turn the creatures of the sea against us. He can blow his horn and cause tidal waves. He could send a tsunami to Paradise Island and destroy everything on it. Drown all of you."

Tears welled up in Robert's eyes. None of this made any sense to him, and yet he knew in his heart it was all true.
"Will I never see you again?"
Irina smiled. "You will. I swear it."
She looked up: "Athena?"

Athena leapt into the water. As the three of them embraced, Irina whispered, "Take care of each other. Know that you are always in my thoughts. And…"

She pulled softly away from them, still holding Robert's hand, "…I'll be watching!"

"I love you, mommy!"

"I love you too, baby girl."

Robert couldn't speak, but held Irina's hand as long as he could… and when her fingertips slid out of his grasp, he held his hand up – *goodbye*. Irina blew him a kiss and disappeared below the surface of the water. Robert instinctively ducked under to look for her, but she was already gone.

# Chapter 30

How many times can a heart break and yet still heal? Do we have the capacity to go through unendurable torment over and over again? Or at some point is it all too much? There's no way to know; life is all about learning the answers to these and a million more questions.

Athena comforted her father as best she could. For days he was nearly inconsolable. Dexter and the others were confused; he'd found Athena, alive and well. It was a miracle. Why did he grieve so?

Athena explained to their friends that coming so close to losing her the same way he'd lost his wife had brought back all of Robert's feelings of loss and grief from eight years earlier. That's why his relief seemed so tinged with sadness. Their friends nodded understandingly and went about their business. That's how it is with friends, sometimes. They were happy to accept a plausible explanation and move on. After all, they had problems of their own.

Athena spent her time talking to her dad, telling him stories of life under the sea. She described Atlantica in minute detail – as minute as she could remember, anyway – and slowly but surely his scientific mind took over. He made copious notes about the culture and the creatures. He created family charts, and researched the mythological history of this not-so-mythological place. He updated the displays in The Dig with the new information Athena had brought back from her adventure.

Slowly, his happiness returned, and once more the sun shone on their lives.

But Athena determined, and Robert agreed, that one day they would go back to Atlantica, and not just for a visit.

They firmly shook hands on this point as Athena said, "We're going to free the humans from slavery, and we're going to bring mom home. And that's a promise."

Athena and Robert began to make confidential plans for this endeavor.

In the mean time, she got a part-time job at Dolphin Cay as a junior trainer. Because of her unique abilities – which she cleverly kept secret from everyone but Robert – she was found to be uncommonly gifted at communicating with the animals. She worked to keep them healthy and strong, and was able to convince them to do all sorts of surprising new tricks. She was extraordinarily helpful to the other trainers as well, and her popularity in Atlantis grew and grew.

She continued to visit with Archibald as often as she could. They picnicked in the grotto, and shared stories of how they spent their week. Archibald brought her the news of Atlantica, and even carried messages back and forth between her and Irina.

Life, as it does, went on.

And sometimes, when the moon was full and hanging low in the sky, Robert and Athena would take a boat out to sea, relax in the cool night breeze and gaze in wonder at the multitude of stars in heaven, while an old sea turtle swam along side, singing songs of days and worlds long gone by.

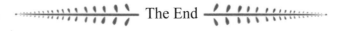 The End

# Acknowledgments

I extend my deepest gratitude to Michele Wiltshire, without whom this book would not exist – literally. I'd also like to thank Errol Cohen and the rest of the Atlantis team for their support.

I'm particularly indebted to my friends Simon Black, Jon Cryer, Ari Frankel, Stephen Kay, Bill Pappalardo and all the other early readers – children and grownups alike – whose feedback and suggestions were enormously useful. Here's to Patricia Galli's 2nd grade class at the Los Feliz Charter School of the Arts, who sat still and listened for two and a half hours!

I'd like to make special mention of Bill Hochhaus and Scott Nash, talented men who offered essential guidance when I was stuck on rocky shoals.

Much appreciation goes to my fellow authors Robert Edelstein, Dave Reisman, Ron Roy and Walt Shiel who generously shared their expertise. I benefited greatly from their hard-learned lessons.

I searched far and wide for the perfect illustrator among dozens of talented people. It was a lucky day when Humberto Braga appeared, and luckier still when he agreed to take on the project. He is a delightful collaborator as well as a tremendously talented artist. I believe he has an enormous career ahead of him.

Love and gratitude go to my family, who have never stopped believing in me and supporting my every endeavor.

Finally, I am happy to acknowledge the contributions of my daughter, Tiger, who truly conceived the story with me. We brainstormed together often, discussing plot points and character traits. She also had valuable input on my choice of illustrator, and insightful opinions about the nature and content of his drawings. One of my greatest joys in bringing this project to fruition has been collaborating with the most important person in my world.

Richard Schenkman is a filmmaker whose movies include "The Pompatus of Love", "Went to Coney Island on a Mission from God... Be Back by Five", "A Diva's Christmas Carol", and "The Man From Earth".

He has worked for MTV, NBC, Nickelodeon, and many other networks.

He has written extensively about cinema, taught writing & directing, and published a fanzine about James Bond 007.

He lives in Los Angeles with his daughter, a cat, and two fish. He loves to scuba dive, but thus far has not conversed with any sea creatures.

This is his first novel.

\*          \*          \*

Humberto Braga has been an artist since birth when he "painted" diapers. His parents confirm that he was quite a handful in his "creative explorations". The shaved dog has never really forgiven him...

He graduated in the Fine Arts from the University of Wisconsin-Waterwater, as well as Media Arts & Animation from the Art Institute of California- San Diego, respectively, with honors.

As a professional artist, he has creatively collaborated with Nickelodeon, MTV, Joseph Kahn, Electronic Arts, among many others.

He lives next to the ocean in California as a freelance artist, a fine art resident at various galleries, and a loving explorer of life, above and below water.

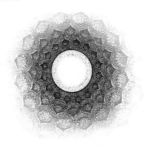